For Per, I love you—T.L.

For my husband Ray. You challenge and inspire me every day. Thank you for your support and for this beautiful life we have made together with our gorgeous girls. Happy 10 year Wedding Anniversary—D.M.

Scholastic Australia
345 Pacific Highway Lindfield NSW 2070
An imprint of Scholastic Australia Pty Limited
PO Box 579 Gosford NSW 2250
ABN 11 000 614 577
www.scholastic.com.au

Part of the Scholastic Group
Sydney • Auckland • New York • Toronto • London • Mexico City
• New Delhi • Hong Kong • Buenos Aires • Puerto Rico

Published by Scholastic Australia in 2016.
Text copyright © Tania Lacy, 2016.
Illustrations copyright © Danielle McDonald, 2016.
Internals various doodles: designs, sketchy, rainbow, groovy, music, G clef, rock © blue67design/
Shutterstock.com; medicine, golf, Australia © Ohn Mar/Shutterstock.com; war doodles © Topform/
Shutterstock.com; borders © Elena Kalistratova/Shutterstock.com; labels © Iriskana/Shutterstock.
com; icons © Merfin/Shutterstock.com; craft © balabolka/Shutterstock.com; school © primiaou/
Shutterstock.com; drum © hchjjl/Shutterstock.com; summer © mhatzapa/Shutterstock.com.

A CiP record for this title is available from the National Library of Australia.

Creator: Lacy, Tania, author.
Title: Tracy Lacy is completely coo-coo bananas! / Tania Lacy ;
Danielle McDonald (illustrator).
ISBN: 9781760156251 (paperback)
Target Audience: For primary school age.
Subjects: Girls--Juvenile fiction.
High schools--Juvenile fiction.
Behavior modification--Juvenile fiction.
Other Creators/Contributors:
McDonald, Danielle, illustrator.
Dewey Number: A823.4

Typeset in Burst My Bubble.

Printed by McPherson's Printing Group, Maryborough, VIC.

Scholastic Australia's policy, in association with McPherson's Printing Group, is to use papers that are renewable and made efficiently from wood grown in responsibly managed forests, so as to minimise its environmental footprint.

10 9 8 7 6 5 4 3 2 1   16 17 18 19 20 / 1

Tracy Lacy

is completely Coo-Coo Bananas !!!!

TANIA LACY

Illustrated by Danielle McDonald

A Scholastic Australia Book

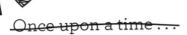

~~Once upon a time . . .~~

~~Once there was a girl. She seemed like a~~
~~normal girl living in a normal home . . .~~

~~It was a dark and stormy night . . .~~

Oh cheesey-cheeses! I'm going to cut straight to
the chase. It's late and I'm still up . . .

. . . and it just keeps coming. Highly unusual because:

1. I'm always too exhausted
   after **ballet class** to be up
   this late.
2. As if I don't have enough
   writing to do for school.
3. Nope. Nothing for number three right now.
   Moving on . . .

So, what could possibly be so urgent, exciting, amazing even, that I'm still awake? I'll tell you **EXACTLY** what it is. I'm **ABSOLUTELY CERTAIN**, well pretty sure, probably about 99.7% sure, that I maybe, nearly, might actually get through high school like A NORMAL PERSON.

Yes I, Tracy Lacy, am a **COCOON** about to become a **butterfly**, an ugly duckling about to become a **beautiful swan**, a tadpole about to become a **frog**. (On that duckling/swan point, I am aware ducklings become ducks, not swans, but in *The Ugly Duckling* story the duck becomes a swan because the duckling is actually a cygnet, but only because the cygnet ... maybe just read the book.) Jeez, in the name of FRONTAL CORTEX OVERLOAD, all these thoughts are coming so quickly my hand can karely beep up with my Brian.

Hold on . . . given this is now an official diary, I need to take care of one small piece of business . . .

To my darling brother Leif, if you even think about reading beyond this page, I will sell my ballet trophies, get a lawyer and sue you for Invasion of Privacy.

signed

NOW WHERE WAS I?

I was here . . . thinking high school was going to be as bleurgh, argh, ungh, ergh and hideously hideous, maybe even HIDEOUS-ER than my primary school days. But now, with just one day of primary school to go, I'm actually looking forward to high school!

I know, I can't believe it either! !?!

Sure, I have to survive the entire summer holidays but I have a plan for that and that plan . . . I'll get back to **THE PLAN**. Right now, all I can say is I haven't been this excited about going to school since . . . my first day of school. Though, thinking back, that wasn't such a great day given that by morning recess I'd realised I'd been **COMPLETELY SCAMMED . . .**

BY MY PARENTS!!!

School is <u>SO</u> much **FUN!**

It's like one big play date!

Teachers are always so nice!

My first day of school

Lies, lies and more lies. And don't even get me started on the whole Tooth Fairy racket they'd been running for years.

I'm still recovering. So who knew my parents would have the know-how to know what to do ... you know?

Sadly primary school has, for me, been plagued by a few **minor events** that meant on the **HA-YA SCALE** ... (HA-YA stands for ☻ow ☻wesome ☻ou ☻re. A stupid scale made up by the so-called 'awesome' kids that—surprise! surprise!—grades how awesome you are. Your awesomeness can be graded anywhere from zero to a trillion, which is ridiculous. Who in the world is a trillion units of awesomeness?) Anyway, according to the **HA-YA SCALE**, I was graded as follows ...

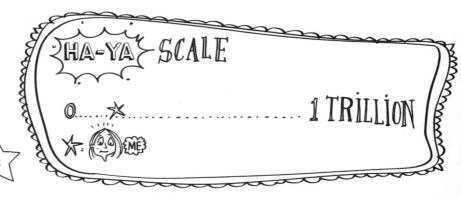

I'd completely understand if you thought this Me person was a complete dodo-bird. But Me is not. Me is fun, Me is bubbly. Once someone even told me, Me has a certain **je ne sais quoi**, which is French for I don't know what. No, it is actually French for I don't know what. What's more, Me is not 'scary-weirdo-alone' kid. Me has friends, the **bestest friends** ever, **Ag** and **Ponky**, and they have stuck by me through everything. **EVERYTHING!**

AG

Ponky

So how is it Me scored so badly on the **HA-YA SCALE?**

Obviously it had something to do with those 'minor events' I mentioned earlier. Some kids remember them as

SOCIALLY CATASTROPHIC,

but you know how kids can exaggerate . . .

OK, they didn't exaggerate, all the stuff that's happened to me, including today's event for which there are no words bad enough to describe—oh wait . . . PERSONALITY FATALITY comes close—is the reason my HA-YA score was so bad. So in hysterical, er, sorry, historical order, the pattern of sadly recurring socially catastrophic events went like this:

1. THE GREAT PINK PONY INCIDENT OF GRADE ONE

I noticed my drawings of spiders, insects, skulls and ghosts never made it onto the art wall, so I decided to draw a **pretty pink pony and a nice rainbow** like all the other girls. I called my pretty pony **Oomphoof**. Our art teacher, Ms Canvass, took issue as to where I'd placed the rainbow.

Oomphoof and the Rainbow

RESULT: Parents called to school for 'a chat'.

'We're all for artistic expression blah, blah, BUT...'

And then I had to put up with everyone making fart noises wherever I went.

Oh ha ha

2. THE GREAT CENSORSHIP INCIDENT OF GRADE TWO

The topic for show-and-tell was 'Did anything out of the ordinary happen at home last night?' Lucky for me it had. My parents had a **terrible fight** over whether potatoes with green skin were poisonous. But then they had a **bath together** and everything was normal again.

Green-skinned potato

I was right in the middle of the story when the teacher ordered me to sit down and not utter **another word.**

RESULT: Parents called to school for discussion about 'inappropriate sharing of information'. I was **banned** from show-and-tell for the rest of the year. My parents told me to **never speak** of baths again.

Jeez, it was just a bath.

3. THE GREAT STRIKE OF GRADE THREE

There is a 'weather policy' that students have spoken of in hushed tones for many moons and it goes like this: When the mercury hits 40 degrees we're to be **SENT HOME**.

40℃ = HOME TIME

So one day when the **temperature** hit the **MAGICAL 40** and we weren't released from the **SAUNA** that was our classroom, everyone decided to strike. Notice the use of the word EVERYONE . Everyone (yes, again with the EVERYONE) made a pact to down tools until we were released.

Miss Grimmett, well known for her temper, looked at us with those beady eyes.

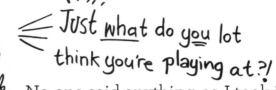

Just _what_ do you lot think you're playing at?!

No-one said anything, so I took it upon myself to let our demands be known. **Courageous and heroic**, I'm sure you'll agree.

'Until we are sent home, as per the **40-degree law**, we are on strike. Right, everyone?'

'GO TRACY! RIGHT ON! YOU TELL HER TRACY!' Well, that's what I expected to hear. Instead, the *tsh-tsh-tsh* of the ceiling fan was all that filled the awkward silence.

We stand here in defiance of oppression

Will you fight?

No

'**RIGHT GUYS?!!?**' *Tsh-tsh-tsh.* OK, the fan was clearly on my side, EVERYONE else however, was too busy copying the lesson from the board!

RESULT: At assembly, Principal Gobjaw announces, 'any ideas of striking or other such recklessness will henceforth be severely punished.'

Any student who assumes she might make the rules around here is quite the WACKADOODLE.

Then EVERYONE (yes EVERYONE)

Wackadoodle!

starts calling me **Wackadoodle**, or **Wacka** for short. Yeah, funny how *NOW* they could speak up.

Wackadoodle

4. THE GREAT PAPER-DART INCIDENT OF GRADE FOUR

You know how you can pull the insides of your pen out and it becomes a **lethal spitball-dart pipe?**

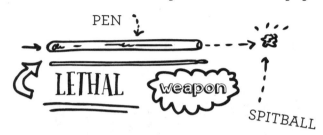

PEN

LETHAL **weapon**

SPITBALL

Well, someone in the class had the bright idea that when the teacher turned her back to write on the board, everyone would **fire spitballs.** But I was late to class so I missed out on the mission details. All I heard was 'NOW!' and within seconds the board and the back of Mrs Roundhouse's head were covered in **spitty bits of paper.**

SPLAT!

'Right, who did that?' Mrs Roundhouse asked, sounding a bit like The Dark Lord. I thought it was the funniest question I'd ever heard. I mean who would be able to fire all those spitballs at machine-gun speed? I laughed out loud. I could afford to, I was innocent.

⚡ BIG MISTAKE! ⚡

'Lacy, Principal's office now!'

'It wasn't me!' I protested.

'Yeah Wacka, just like it wasn't you who tried to make us all go on strike?' Brad Cunningham, or 'Cunners' as he was known, piped up, obviously the mastermind behind the attack.

RESULT: So much for me being the Wackadoodle!

P.S. I only took the rap to avoid being on **CUNNERS'
HOT LIST.** If I dobbed him in, my life would be
a **gazillion times** worse. Cunners was the kid who
started the whole HA-YA SCALE because everyone,
including Cunners, thinks he is the **one trillion units of
awesomeness** they want to be. And why wouldn't they?
Tall, good-looking, charming enough to fool any teacher,
but ratbaggy enough to
earn the respect of the boys
and crushes from the girls.
My crush-less relationship
with Cunners had caused
an unspoken rift. He **didn't
fool me.**

BRAD
'You don't fool me'
CUNNERS

5. THE GREAT FAIRYTALE INCIDENT OF GRADE FIVE

Not so much an incident as a ton of incidents ... I had become a living fairytale, and not the happily ever after Cinderella type. It was destined to happen, I suppose. Stories of the dumb things I'd done were being passed down from student to student, told and re-told, again and again and again.

A living fairytale

And again and again, and they haunted me every which way I turned. Grade One kids would ask if I really drew a rainbow-farting pony. Grade Two kids asked if I was actually banned from show-and-tell and so on and so on. BUT ... what made me CRAZY IN THE COCONUT about all this is no-one ever talked about the good stuff I did, just like {CINDERELLA} ! See, I have a theory about Cinderella ... in my Cinderella Fairytale, this girl is a GO-GETTER! A DOER! A BORN SURVIVOR!

How else would she have lived through her terrible existence? Think about it, one minute she's a **slave** to her ugly step-sisters, the next she's **married to a prince**, who, though destined to become King, has never lifted a finger in his life ... except maybe to preen his glorious head of hair. So my ending to this fairytale goes like this ... Cinderella quickly realises her prince has no idea how to run a country but has plenty of **potential in hairdressing**. She knows something has to be done and given she's used to hard work ... **darn the consequences** thinks Cinderella, and off to university she goes.

UGLY STEP-sisters

She gets a **Degree in Economics** and then lives happily ever after because she is a really clever, outspoken woman and her husband loves her for that.

But all anyone ever dreams of is Cinderella riding off with the prince. Like that's some kind of achievement!??! No-one thinks she might have done something amazing with her life, just like no-one ever thinks about my **AMAZING** straight-A (except for art where I maintain a consistent D) report card.

> But I do have a degree in Economics. Who do you think runs this country?

RESULT: The lesson here is this . . . it's not just in fairytales that the Handsome Prince trumps the Economics Degree. I've learnt that in real life, Dumb Acts trump (almost) Straight As. People put value in some coo-coo story before actual smarts, every time.

There's something very wrong with this picture.

6. THE FINAL 'THERE ARE NO WORDS TO DESCRIBE HOW BAD THIS WAS' EMBARRASSMENT OF GRADE SIX

Now, before we get to the 'event for which there are no words bad enough to describe', I have to say Grade Six had been relatively INCIDENT FREE. There were a couple of close shaves, like the time we were in art class . . . of course.

It was near Halloween and Ms Canvass said she wanted to see something 'ghoulish' on the page. But what I heard was 'goulash' . . . as in Dad's favourite casserole. And yes, I did think it was a weird request but given my history with Ms Canvass, I was not about to ask any questions. When Ponky saw my big bowl of steaming goulash—which definitely wasn't 'ghoulish' but was definitely the best drawing I had ever done—quick as a flash he swapped our drawings and put his name on mine just seconds before

PONKY

Ms Canvass arrived at our table. Boy, did she lose it. 'Oh, how funny! Now get out!' she yelled, obviously thinking Ponky was taking her for a ride. She even made him stay after class, lecturing him on the importance of carrying out her instructions properly. It was becoming obvious that Ms Canvass wasn't a big fan of artistic interpretation. Anyways, it turned out to be a win for Ponky. Sure, he did it for me and sure he got into trouble, but somehow, improbably, the boys suddenly saw him as a bit of a hero. He even moved up the HA-YA SCALE. Go figure.

The long and the short of all this was yes, there had been 'incidents' in Grade Six but I'd not suffered the embarrassment of years gone by. But only because I'd been saved by Ag and Ponky or I was lucky enough to run away before anyone saw anything incriminating. So I thought YES! Finally I was FREE! FREE I TELL YOU! FREE FROM THE SHACKLES OF MY PAST!

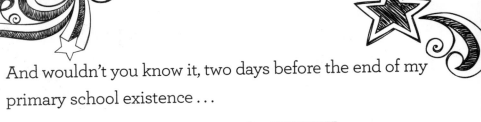

And wouldn't you know it, two days before the end of my primary school existence ...

MY LIFE IS A DISASTER!!!!

There I was daydreaming my way through art class, as I often did because I'd realised even if I had the **talent of Vincent van Gogh** and I cut off my ear, Ms Canvass would probably give me detention for bleeding to death on her floor. (She's never forgiven me for the entire Oomphoof fiasco ... I was in Grade One for goodness sake!) Anyway, suddenly ... the weirdest thing happened. **OOMPHOOF APPEARED** right outside the window! There she was in all her glory, with her **beautiful butt-rainbow**, which smelt like strawberries and blueberries with a slight whiff of off-egg. Oomphoof was so happy to see me but I knew why she was there. This was goodbye. We were both moving on.

'Yo Tracy Lacy, don't go changin'!' she said. And then she let out this almighty ...

24

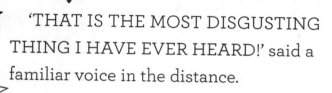

BUUUURRRᵣᵣRP

'THAT IS THE MOST DISGUSTING THING I HAVE EVER HEARD!' said a familiar voice in the distance.

But I was so excited by what had happened, I blurted it out for all to hear,

Look! Oomphoof just spewed up lollies covered in pink horsey-spit!

And everyone was laughing, sharing in this joyous moment ... and that's when I **snapped to**.

That familiar voice? Ms Canvass.

That burp? Me.

That laughter? **THE TSUNAMI OF RIDICULE** I had unleashed. I froze as everyone pointed and laughed. Even Ms Canvass was looking at me smugly, like she'd been waiting for this moment ever since she'd laid eyes on my beautiful Oomphoof. And so, I did the only thing a girl in my position could do . . .

RUN!!!!

SEE TRACY RUN . . .

I ran out of that classroom, past the front gates, just as the most important realisation I have ever had slapped me about the face and donged me on the head:

There was no way **A GIRL LIKE ME** would make it through **high school** alive!!!

(Let alone **TOMORROW!!!** MY VERY LAST DAY of primary school EVER!)

Brain working overtime. Choices. Options. Plans. Needed now. Not just now, NOW!

SIDE-THOUGHT: Tell Mum and Dad TODAY was the last day of school. **SOLVED!** END SIDE-THOUGHT

SIDE-SIDE-THOUGHT: But tomorrow is going to be just one day of hell. If I don't do something, I'm facing **SIX YEARS** of **HELL** in **HIGH SCHOOL!!!!** END SIDE-SIDE-THOUGHT

SIDE-SIDE-SIDE-THOUGHT:

I HATE ART CLASS

END SIDE-SIDE-SIDE-THOUGHT

Wahh

By the time I got home I was past crying and well into the sobbing stage, that kind where you can only get one word out at a time. Mum and Dad were all ears even if they couldn't make out what I was saying.

'You (uh) have (uh) to (uh) home (uh) school me! (uh-uh)!'

SOBBING

And who would have thought my parents, yes those people from last century, would have the answer to my problem.

WOLFGANG

My dad, Wolfgang, is German but is bizarrely a complete softie. If his kids are upset, he's upset. 'I get ze tiss-use, you vill need zem. I, of course do not ... **VHERE ARE (UH) ZE SCHTUPID TISS-(UH-UH)-USEZ!!!!**'

My mum, Margaret, not German, is a little less patient with emotional outbursts.

Just wipe that snot on your sleeve and get on with it.

(You get the picture.)

MARGARET
(NOT German)

'All primary (uh) school has taught (uh) me is that I'm (uh-uh) **COMPLETELY COO-COO BANANAS!** Oomphoof proved it!' Tears follow, sobbing, sobbing, more sobbing until finally Dad pulled himself together.

'Oomphoof?!! Vhat is zis Oomphoof?'

Activated ALMOND Milk

To which Mum added, 'Have you been drinking that activated almond milk?' Mum is convinced it sends me loopy and the hippy mums who run the canteen put something in it to make us

Hippy mum

kids more 'relaxed'. Mum kept going on and on about the hippy mums and their **MIND-CONTROL FOOD MOVEMENT** until finally I'd had enough.

'I don't care about the hippy mums! We're moving to the outback and I'm doing School of the Air and that's the end of it!!!'

I was waiting for 'go to your room' when Dad said, 'Oont now vee are moofing to zee owtback all because my dawter is a soshall owtkast??!!?'

OK, I wouldn't have gone that far but ...

'She's not a social outcast, Wolf. You, my darling girl, simply march to the beat of a different drum.'

The beat of a different drum?!! Was she for real?

SIDE-THOUGHT: Cross 'Marching Band' off list of possible career options. END SIDE-THOUGHT

UNGH, I hate it when Mum gets all mum-like with her weirdo mum-isms.

CLASSIC MUM-ISMS OF ME SO FAR INCLUDED:

You hear classical when everyone else hears heavy metal.

You're the comic book in the literature section.

A snowball in a bonfire.

A WALNUT AMONGST DOUGHNUTS.

You're the live cow in the activated almond milk section.

The banjo player in an orchestra.

I know, weird, right? And here she was rambling on **AGAIN!** 'Maybe you need to look at this experience in a different way. Sometimes good things do come out of bad things, so . . .'

ZAP! Before she finished the sentence my brain SUDDENLY made sense of EVERYTHING she'd been saying all these years. Maybe it was the marching to the beat that did it. She had spoken to the dancer in me. I don't fit in but if fitting in, thus, therefore and ipso facto, surviving high school, was as simple as walking to the same beat of the same drum, as in left, right, left, right, 1, 2, 3, 4, my chances of doing so just increased by 200%. I am a dancer, so am obviously very coordinated and obviously able to march ... in time, what's more.

... left, right, left, right ...

It was all so clear now. I had gone through primary school dancing a polka, which is more of a 'hop-1-2-3, hop-1-2-3' when all I had to do was march to the beat of the same drum! Parrum-par-par-pum! I mean, left, right, left, right, 1, 2, 3, 4.

POLKA

Mum was right! (Now there's a sentence I never thought I'd write.) Maybe good things <u>do</u> come out of bad. Oomphoof's visit today was the very thing I needed because it showed me it's a very fine line between **bananas** (er . . . drawing pink ponies) and **completely coo-coo bananas** (pink rainbow-farting ponies called Oomphoof visiting you at the art-room window).

Bottom line: mythical creatures do not fart rainbows or vomit candy.

NO farting rainbows

NO candy VOMIT

Bottom-bottom line: **bananas** is fine but **completely coo-coo bananas** is **definitely not** fine. And now that I know that, **I AM GOING TO FIX IT!** And that's where **THE PLAN** comes in. I'm pretty sure **THE PLAN** is the good thing that's come out of the bad thing.

Morning TL, all very interesting. Just wanted to let you know your ballet trophies aren't real gold. They're not even gold-plated, they're plastic gold. Good luck finding a lawyer who'll work for that.

Aaaargh! I HATE YOU Leif.

Come near my diary again and I will unleash a world of pain upon you. Yes, a world of pain, Leif!

More painful than:

When you put the very special sprinkles on my cupcake . . . the special 'hottest in the world' Chilli Flake sprinkles!!

MY TONGUE!

How you said putting my tongue in the freezer would cool it down.

When you told me that stepping on the rake had been scientifically proven as the best way to improve a dancer's reflexes.

And that there was no way an AA-sized battery could electrocute me . . .

More painful than all of that combined, Leif.

Signed,

 Tracy 'I REALLY MEAN IT' Lacy

Hang on. Why am I wasting my time on stupid Leif and his stupid stuff when I should be celebrating?

TODAY IS THE LAST DAY OF PRIMARY SCHOOL EVER!

BUT FIRST, A MOMENT TO REWIND PLEASE . . .

Yesterday, all my hoo-ha with drums, polkas and the brain zap got me thinking, so I rang Ag and Ponky the second I knew they'd be back from school.

'DEUM!' I said. That's our special code—Drop Everything Urgent Meeting.

Once the code word is spoken it's NEGI—No Excuses Go Immediately.

Shortly after, there we stood, we three, dwarfed by the gates of Northwood High, soon to be our home away from home.

'Hear that?' I said. 'That is the sound of angels singing!'

LAAAAAAAAAAAAAAAA!

Ag wanted to know if I'd been drinking the activated almond milk, 'cos she couldn't hear anything. (Jeez, her and my mother!)

'LISTEN HARDER!' I said. 'THESE ARE NO ORDINARY ANGELS,' I said. 'THESE ARE THE ANGELS OF NEW BEGINNINGS, REINVENTION AND FULLY COMPREHENSIVE AWESOMENESS,' I said. **'AND RIGHT NOW THEY ARE SENDING US A VERY IMPORTANT MESSAGE!!!!'**

Ponky asked if I wouldn't mind passing on their message 'cos all he could hear was me shouting. As clearly and kindly as I could, I explained. 'Going to high school is the perfect opportunity for us to become better us's. If we are to stand any chance of survival, or moving up the HA-YA SCALE . . .' (on which, as you might expect, we have all ended up with majorly dud scores) . . .

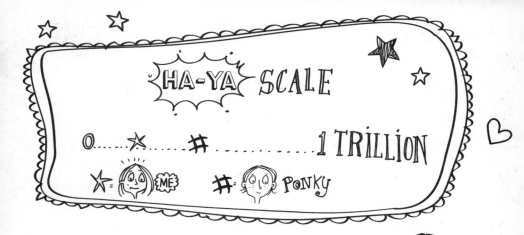

PLEASE NOTE: You will see Ag did not score at all. This is because she is **part ninja**, I'm sure of it. Not a deathly sword-wielding ninja, but a 'suddenly she's there, has been there for ages but you didn't notice her' ninja. Three times this term she was marked absent when she was actually at school. But back to the very important speech I was making...

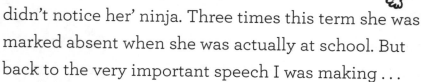

'We need to make **serious personal changes** so we can walk through the gates of **high school**, confident we are **walking** to the **beat** of the **socially accepted drum**.'

It took some time for Ag and Ponky to get their heads around the drum concept but once I demonstrated the march as opposed to the polka they got it. But can you believe it? They were totally against the idea. Apparently they are quite happy with who they are.

'Mwah-ha-ha-ha-ha,' I laughed crazily, which kind of even scared me, but as I explained, 'We won't be dealing with primary school kids anymore. We will be walking into a slaughterhouse, that's right, a **SLAUGHTERHOUSE** of bigger kids with hormones and stuff that make them **ACT CRAZY**. And who knows what those hormones will do to us! We need to be ready! That's why I have developed

THE PLAN.

'Yay, a plan. Thank goodness there's a plan!' Ag and Ponky squealed as they jumped for joy.

At least that's what I thought would happen. But no, they just stared at me. Worse still, it was the 'wacka stare'. From them! MY BEST FRIENDS!

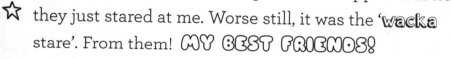

THE WACKA STARE

'Oh come on! All we have to do is spend the entire summer holiday working on any personal flaws that would make us easy prey to the "walking to the beat of the same drum" wolves who hunt "polka-dancing" smaller mammals such as ourselves.' Then . . . Ag and Ponky actually pooh-poohed my entire theory!

'If we don't make a good impression right from the very start of high school, the next six years of our lives will be SOCIAL TORMENT!'

Suddenly they were all ears. The more dramatic approach was definitely the way to go.

'I don't want any of us devoured by wolves or hanging off a butcher's hook!'

Now they were *hanging off* my every word.

'Thus, therefore and ipso facto, the need for THE PLAN.'

Yes! They were in! Sacred spit was spat, spit-hands were shaken, the deal was made ... and I hadn't even told them THE PLAN. Now that's commitment!

P-t-t-t!

'And so,' I continued, 'THE PLAN is ... tonight, we each write a list of the AREAS OF IMPROVEMENT we think each other needs to work on.'

'So basically a list of anything we find annoying about each other,' Ponky said.

'Yes, anything annoying. Anything at all. We will meet before school to share the lists.' I noted Ag and Ponky swapping a nervous glance. In the name of HOLEY SWISS CHEESES! What now? Turns out Ag and Ponky were worried about me going to school tomorrow after the 'event for which there are no words bad enough to describe'. (Awww, my friends.)

'Well, I've nothing to lose anymore so I might as well face the music, which I imagine will be something in the death metal genre. **I am certain** by the time we start high school, the "event for which there are no words bad enough to describe" will be forgotten! Well, mostly . . . hopefully . . . nearly.'

'And because of **THE PLAN**, nothing as **cataclysmically cataclysmical** as the "event for which there are no words bad enough to describe" will ever happen to any of us again! **I JUST KNOW IT!!!**' Then we group-hugged.

HAPPINESS.

LAST DAY OF PRIMARY SCHOOL EVER!

I was out that door faster than you could say 'Our entire lives are going to change *for the better*, and there is nothing anyone can do to stop us, not even superheroes because by the time we have enacted "THE PLAN" we are going to be the superheroes in this legendary tale of superhero-ness and . . .'

Oh, I was already at the meeting point so I guess the rest of that will have to wait for another day.

There we stood, **DWARFED** again by the gates of **Northwood High**, lists in hand.

THE GREAT LIST EXCHANGE...

The air was thick with a sense of ceremony... or so I thought. I was soon to discover it wasn't ceremony I was sensing. I should have **TWIGGED** when I handed my lists to Ag and Ponky and they started saying maybe this **wasn't such a great idea.** Looking back, I was just too excited to be reading the very obvious signs they were giving off.

'Just get on with it! This is **lifesaving** stuff!' I said, my heart beating a million miles an hour **BECAUSE** I knew what helpful-goodful stuff I had written in **my lists.**

AG – AREAS FOR IMPROVEMENT

FROM TRACY

1. **NO MORE** going **unnoticed**, it's an **EASY** way out.

2. You **MUST** find your 'don't mess with ME attitude' and access it frequently. *Refer point 1*

3. Speak **UP**, speak **OUT**, let people see who you are. *Again refer point 1*

Finally {AG} I would just like to add, I love you very much so embrace change or **DIE**.

Lots of *Love* Tracy xx

PONKY AREAS FOR IMPROVEMENT

FROM TRACY

1. We are **NOT** mind-readers, express your feelings.

② You are **too OLD** to be sulking when you don't get your way.
Refer point ①.

③ Holding grudges makes you **UNAPPEALING**. REFER POINT ①

We have known **each other** since we were babies. I feel I can tell you this with love . . .

Don't even think about **sulking** when you get this letter.

♡ Lots of love. ♡

Tracy
x x x

I was very proud of the balance of gentle but firm advice I'd given ... until Ag and Ponky gave their notes to each other ...

PONKY

AREAS for **IMPROVEMENT**

from **AG**

You are very supportive. But you don't have to be supportive all the time. I think this will help you improve as a person.

Ag-areas for improvement - from **Ponky**

Please don't take this the wrong way. You are very nice. Maybe you could improve by being even nicer.

SERIOUSLY?

Obviously I had not made the point of the exercise clear. And obviously there would be nothing on their lists that would help me. Interestingly enough, they then handed me a combined list. At least they'd put some thought into it. But with the benefit of hindsight ... this was not a good sign. Again with the 'hindsight thing', if anyone ever hands you a list with the heading AREAS FOR IMPROVEMENT and it unfurls like a roll of toilet paper, this is also not a good sign.

AREAS of IMPROVEMENT for TRACY

(REMEMBER YOU DID SAY <u>ANYTHING ANNOYING</u>)

1. You have to stop putting on plays for the class.
2. You have to stop doing the splits up the wall.
3. You never listen to advice.
4. You always have to have the last word.
5. You need to think before you speak.
6. You are bossy.
7. You talk too much.
8. You talk over people.
9. You say 'ipso facto' and no-one knows what it means.
10. You try too hard to make people like you.
11. You argue with anyone who doesn't agree with you.

12. You daydream and talk out loud which makes you look crazy.

13. You think it's your duty to speak for 'everyone'. It's not.

14. You share too much information.

15. You expect praise for every little thing you do.

16. You make every little thing a drama.

17. You spend too much time thinking about fitting in.

18. You're always so busy with ballet and sometimes you forget about us.

19. You should be happy with who you are.

Nineteen? They couldn't round it off at **twenty?**
Really? Anyway, what happened next was all a bit
murky. All I remember is, short of putting on a quick
play and doing the splits up the wall, everything that
came out of my mouth confirmed everything they'd
listed. And it went a little like this . . .

Me: I can't believe you did this!
(points **3, 5 & 16**)

Ponky: It was your idea. We
warned you.

Me: But half this stuff isn't true! (point **3**)

AG & Ponky: YES IT IS!

Me: If anyone read this they'd think I
was a complete nutbag! (points **3, 16**)

AG: Don't be sill—

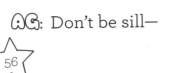

Me: And when do I ever talk over people? (point **8**)

Ponky: Practically all the—

Me: And not taking advice? Give me one example. (points **8, 11**)

Ponky: This stupid list for starters.

Me: That is the dumbest thing I have ever heard! IPSO FACTO, not a valid point. (points **5, 9, 11**) I was doing this to help all of us. (points **10, 13**)

AG: But you're the one not listening!

Me: OK, this argument is over. (points **3, 4, 6**) This is the worst day of my life! (point **16**) If only Oomphoof

were here and we could ride away into the sunset. Though I have to do something about that rainbow coming out of her butt. No, darn it, I will not. I can put a rainbow wherever I like. (point **12**)

AG: Trace?

Me: What? Oh right. Yes, this is over! Maybe forever! (points **4, 16**)

Me: But I'll have to think about it. (point **4**)

And then we walked to school in **silence**. Not the happy celebratory celebration 'last ever walk to primary school EVERRRRRRRRRRRRRRRR!' I was hoping for.

SIDE-THOUGHT: I was being an **IDIOT**. END SIDE-THOUGHT

MEANWHILE, IN THE CLASSROOM TIME PORTAL . . .

Without going into too much
detail, the rest of the morning of
the very last day of primary school
EVERRRRRRRRRRRRRRRRR

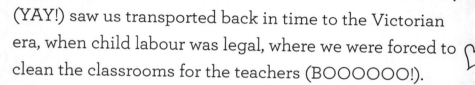

(YAY!) saw us transported back in time to the Victorian
era, when child labour was legal, where we were forced to
clean the classrooms for the teachers (BOOOOOO!).

Turns out even in Victorian times teasing was
ye popular pastime for ye children of ye day. Yes,
everyone seized whatever opportunity they could to
laugh and poke fun at me over 'the event for which
there are no words bad enough to describe'. Not like I
wasn't expecting it. Not like it didn't cut to the bone or
anything. All I kept repeating was THE PLAN, THE
PLAN but as you can imagine, even that was hanging
by a thread, what with Ag and Ponky and me not really
speaking. So much for nothing to lose.

OH, HOW THINGS CAN CHANGE . . .

There we were, me, Ag and Ponky in the middle of the school hall wondering how in the name of bubblegum could this have happened. (Oh, just so you know, we were on speaking terms by now, though the AREAS FOR IMPROVEMENT topic was definitely a no-go zone at this point in time.)

But back to the topic at hand . . . It was a tragic tragedy, without doubt the most disastrous disaster the school had ever seen and I doubted it would ever recover from the dismal sight that was our . . .

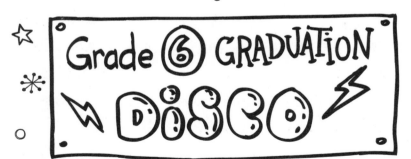

Grade ⑥ GRADUATION DISCO

So let me paint the picture of what we walked into.

In one corner a group of girls were hugging, making this weird EEEE-OO-ARGH-ARGH sound, which sounded exactly like a tribe of monkeys in a restaurant fighting over the menu.

Turns out that EEEE-OO-ARGH-ARGH sound was them crying. The girls, not the monkeys. As if monkeys would sit in a restaurant crying.

Then again, it's not entirely impossible.

Some of the guys were in a football huddle trying to look macho but their heaving shoulders were a dead giveaway. They were crying too? This was unbelievable!

Everyone else was dotted around the hall, leaning against walls or sitting hopelessly on the floor, all staring into space.

Had we just walked into a . . .

ZOMBIE

Snippets of conversation wafted our way.

I'm gonna miss how you **BOSS** us around.

I'm gonna miss how you **TALK** about me behind my **BACK**.

If only we could **STAY** in primary school **FOREVER**.

I'm gonna **MISS** your **ATOMIC WEDGIES**

I'm gonna miss your **FARTS** 'cos they smell like **POPCORN!**

Me too, 'cos my mum doesn't let me eat **POPCORN**.

This whole scene needed fixing and fast!

'People, people, people! Have I just walked into a funeral?' I said, 'Let's turn those frowns upside down and get this party started!'

Let's get this **PARTY** started!

Inspiring right? Perfect way to lighten the mood. WRONG!

SHUT UP **TRACY** LACY!

The voice seemed to come from the tribe of monkeys. Oh no... VICTORIA FULLER! Victoria... think tall, sporty, strong (respect) but mean, really mean (un-respect). Also well known for her catchphrase,

WHOOP! WHOOP! WHOOP! LET'S GO!

It's kind of annoying, not that any of that really mattered right now because she was heading straight for me AND she didn't look happy AND that look could only mean ONE thing ... 'You are dead meat!' or possibly TWO things ... 'You are dead meat and you are going down!' But by the way her fist was clenched, I'm pretty sure it meant 'I am going to ram my fist in your mouth so you will never say another dumb thing in your life!' I closed my eyes, braced myself and even opened my mouth so as to make her job easier.

Hey, Icki, yanna hih uh 'ance 'oor?

THEN the most amazing thing happened ...

I was there with my mouth open ready for Victoria Fuller to rip out my larynx. But she didn't. Instead she got right up in my face shouting like a platoon sergeant. But given the stink of her breath, I almost wish she'd gone with larynx removal. *Beetroot!* She'd been eating *beetroot* ... or was it *dirt*? I think it was *dirt*! I wouldn't be surprised if Victoria took a lunch box full of dirt to school. She's so into sport she'd probably eat it for its iron content or something. But back to Victoria, right up in my face with her dirt breath ...

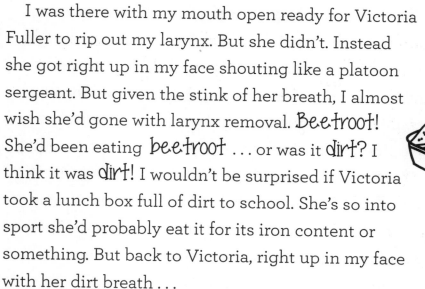

CAN'T YOU SEE THIS IS NO TIME FOR DANCING! WE'RE ALL GOING TO DIFFERENT HIGH SCHOOLS. I, FOR EXAMPLE, WILL BE GOING TO A PRIVATE SCHOOL SO WILL PROBABLY NEVER MIX WITH MY PEOPLE AGAIN. WE THOUGHT WE'D BE BFFS FOREVER!!

And then I laughed.

I LAUGHED? **I LAUGHED!!!**

I was trying to hold it in but it snuck out my nose, 'Nnnuuunnngh . . .'

'Oh, you think this is funny, Tracy? Tracy who sees imaginary ponies outside the window?'

'Yes, I will admit to the pony, whose name is OOMPHOOF by the way, but no, I don't think what you're talking about is funny. But I do think "BFFs forever" is funny because if you think about it, it actually means "Best Friends Forever Forever". Ag and me and Ponky talk about this stuff all the time, don't we guys? Guys? It's like ATM machine, "Automatic Teller Machine" machine. I mean, anyone can see that's just plain idiotic, right? BUT, you want to know something Victoria Fuller . . .'

And right at that moment, what POPS into my HEAD? Points 5, 7, 13, 14, 16. Ag and Ponky were right on the money! My head wanted to keep going and show Miss Victoria 'WHOOP! WHOOP! WHOOP!

LET'S GO!' Fuller who was right, but my heart knew if I really wanted to change, now was as good a time as any to start. But could I? And then this came out . . .

'But you want to know something Victoria Fuller . . . *you're right.* I've been so **inconsiderate** and I'm **REALLY SORRY**. And I'm really going to miss you. In fact, I'll miss everyone that won't be going on to Northwood High.'

But you want to know something VICTORIA FULLER . . . you're right.

Well, Ag and Ponky looked like this . . .

And Victoria Fuller looked like this . . .

Then like this . . .

'You trying to be clever?' she asked.

This was actually a very difficult question because the truth was I **was** trying to be clever by seizing this moment to change the faults my friends had so accurately pointed out. But if I said yes, it could come across as point 4. And if I answered no, it could be point 10, possibly leading to point 16. So I didn't say anything. Victoria was really confused but so was I. This had never happened... **ON MY ENTIRE LIFE!** Then Victoria turned to everyone in the hall ...

Oh great, I thought, **more** pink pony jokes. I decided I would ...

1. Brace myself for the put-downs.

2. Turn to Ag and Ponky and admit this 'change' thing was my dumbest idea ever.

3. Still nothing for number three.

'Tracy's right!' Victoria said. 'We need to **PARRRRTAAAAAY! WHOOP! WHOOP! WHOOP! LET'S GO!**' And then everyone hit the dance floor!!

WHOOP! WHOOP! WHOOP! LET'S GO!

WHAT. JUST. HAPPENED?

I was a hero is what just happened! I got that party started. Wait, **everyone thinks Victoria Fuller** got the party started. Everyone thinks . . . that's not how . . . it was my . . .

'THAT WAS MY IDEA!' I screamed. But nobody heard me. With the music so loud and everyone too busy patting Victoria 'champion of the dancing people' on the back, I just looked like a crazy mime artist.

Ag and Ponky, being the amazing friends they are, were still by my side. 'Point 15, right?' They nodded, I smiled. And then I realised that while I may have missed my chance to go out a hero, this change idea REALLY WORKED! I'd just proved it.

I knew it. They knew it.

'Do I need to say I told you so?' I asked. Our group hug proved I didn't. 'From this moment forward **THE PLAN** will be known as...

OPERATION BETTER US'S

and OPERATION BETTER US'S IS GO!'

Then me, Ag and Ponky danced like there was no more primary school ever!

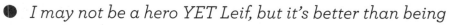
Hero? You? BAHAHAHAHAHAHA! I'm telling Mum you've lost your na-na.

I may not be a hero YET Leif, but it's better than being King of the Dorks ... your Majest-dork!

COMMENCE COUNTDOWN

♡ Day 1 of **SUMMER** holidays ♡

♡ 42 days to start of HIGH SCHOOL ♡

♡ 5 days to CHRISTMAS ♡

COMMENCE OPERATION BETTER US'S

TASK 1 OF 2

Ponky and I went to the library
(incredibly last century, I know) and
borrowed some self-help books. Turns
out self-help books are exactly what
they say they are, books you use to
help yourself. They have names like
How to Be a Better You, You
Can Be Better, BETTER YOU, YOU
BETTER, You Are You . . . But Better.

Most of them are written by real doctors though I'm not so sure about *Dr Mum*. Ponky said we should steer clear of anything with 'Mum' on the front cover anyway 'cos his mum reckons there's no degree in parenting.

'What?!!? They're just making this stuff up as they go along???'

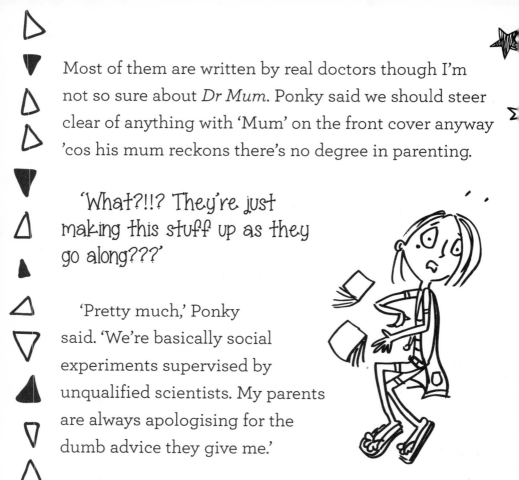

'Pretty much,' Ponky said. 'We're basically social experiments supervised by unqualified scientists. My parents are always apologising for the dumb advice they give me.'

First of all, his parents actually apologise when they make mistakes? And second of all, this whole 'parenting' thing is just another scam grown-ups are running?

'Thank goodness we've taken things into our own hands,' Ag said, scaring the bejingo out of us.

She'd been there the whole time! (We need to find a self-help book on deprogramming ninjas before this girl gives someone a heart attack.) We left the library with our arms full of books, ensuring we were not seen by anyone because obviously . . .

SCHOOL HOLIDAYS + LIBRARY VISIT x ARMS FULL OF BOOKS = MAJOR NERD STATUS

Back at Ponky's, we divided up the books. Now all we had to do was read, absorb and wait for the change to wash over us. We would meet again to discuss our progress.

TASK 2 OF 2   SURVIVE CHRISTMAS

Christmas shopping done, now I wait for the drama to build, leading to a **nuclear-sized** explosion on Christmas Day. See, my dad **LOVES** Christmas. If he could get a job as one of Santa's elves he would. I guess coming from Germany, the inventors of the Christmas tree, it's in his blood. Meanwhile, my mum **HATES** Christmas. Hate might be too strong a word, but she does get very, very, very . . .

STRESSED!

Mum says it's because Grandma is a big know-all. And she is, she knows so, so much, about everything which I thought would make Mum proud. She's always telling Mum how to do things a better way or a different way or her way. Mum can't see Grandma's just trying to help. So Mum starts shouting at Grandma and Grandma shouts at Mum and then Leif and I start shouting, mostly things like **pass the peas** otherwise no-one hears you and you go hungry, then Dad starts shouting for everyone to **stop shouting** and then lunch is over.

And don't even get me started on how Dad insists we have a traditional German Christmas Feast of **roast goose!!! (BLEURGH!)** So there we sit, locked inside the house, air conditioners blasting, because, of course, it's usually 40 degrees outside, wishing we could just once have a barbecue like everyone else in Australia.

★ MAJOR SIDE-THOUGHT: PROBABLY MOST MAJOR SIDE-THOUGHT EVER: POSSIBLY 'ALERT THE MEDIA' SIZED SIDE-THOUGHT:

I've just realised our **entire family** is Completely Coo-Coo Bananas. **WHAT CHANCE DID I HAVE?** With coo-coo genes on both sides of the family, I was a sitting banana.

END MAJOR SIDE-THOUGHT: PROBABLY MOST MAJOR SIDE-THOUGHT EVER: POSSIBLY 'ALERT THE MEDIA' SIZED SIDE-THOUGHT.

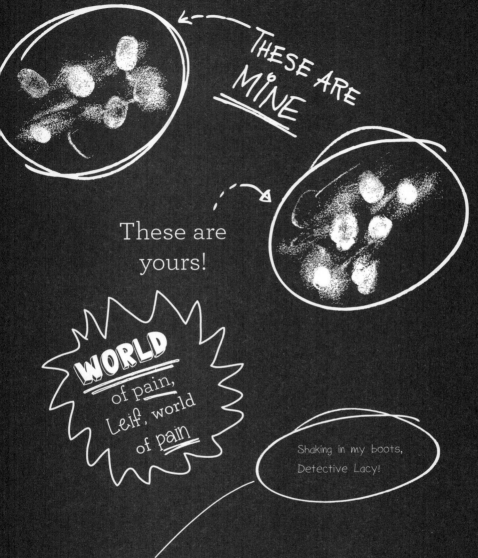

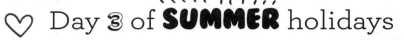

Day **3** of **SUMMER** holidays

40 days to start of **HIGH SCHOOL**

3 days to CHRISTMAS

DISASTER!!

AG

ME

So, after a great day hanging at Ponky's pool with Ag ... did I mention Ponky lives next door and is exactly three-months-to-the-day older than me? It was me who called him Ponky because inky, pinky, ponky ... he stunk! And just like a bad smell, the name has hung around. Something else that was so cute when we were little is that Ponky would tell everyone he was going to marry me. Ten years on, he's still saying it. It's not so cute anymore. Ponky's parents are really good friends with my parents so we all get together for barbecues and stuff.

LEIF

But back to the **DISASTER**. I walked in the door and there's Leif ... smirking. 'Mum and Dad want to see you in ...

THE LOUNGE
(DA-DA DA DAAAAA!)

(Beethoven's 5th in case anyone was wondering.)

THE LOUNGE (DA-DA DA DAAAAA!)

is a room that exists purely because Mum wanted a formal lounge, just because she wanted one, which is otherwise never used, except for family talks, so I wasn't surprised when I walked into ...

THE <u>LOUNGE</u> (DA-DA DA DAAAAA!)

... and Mum said,

We NEED to have a FAMILY TALK

Was this THE talk or A talk? Who cares, both were crappy options. And then horror of all horrificly horrifying horrors ... Mum pulled out the self-help books I had hidden under my bed. LEIF! Who else but LEIF?!

Two jobs, two! That's all an older sibling is born to do. If they do nothing else their entire life, fine, so long as they ...

1. Break down the walls, forge a path, push the boundaries so as to make an easy road for the younger child and . . .

2. Never break the secret sibling covenant of any trouble, plans or stuff that would lead to punishment or concern BY TELLING YOUR PARENTS!!

So far, any wall-breaking, path-forging and boundary-pushing has been left to me. And while I do not have any dirt on my brother, I would never tell Mum and Dad if I did. It's an outrage! A crime against sibling-ty!

Mum and Dad fired questions my way thick and fast.

Tell us vhat is happent so vee can help you.

Leif said you'd been saying some strange things.

Why didn't you come to us if you needed help?

He sinks you haff gone craissey!

85

UNNNNNGGH! Why couldn't they see he was the evil genius behind this whole ambush! All I could hear in my mind was '**think** Tracy, **think**!'. I started talking hoping something would come to me . . .

'Oh, those . . . yeah, I was reading them because . . .' THINK! THINK! . . . **0 THUNK OT!!** ' . . . they're on the pre-reading list for "Education For Living".'

Blank stares from Mum and Dad. Good, this is where you want them to be, buying you time to invent the rest of your story . . .

BLANK STARES

'One of my subjects at **high school**? The place I will be attending in forty days?' 40 days! Gak! Time was slipping away and I hadn't done any work. I grabbed my books, garbling something about getting onto this right away, running straight for my room.

Mum yelled after me, 'What's "Education For Living"?'

'It's um ... where some old teacher-guy stands there and says how in his day you could buy a giant bag of lollies for twenty cents.'

In my day . . .

Some old teacher-guy

OK, not my best work but if I've heard it once I've heard it a million times from the people of last century. What I think they're trying to say is the smaller the lolly bag, the worse life is. And that's the closest I've ever come to learning anything about life BC (Before Computers) and life PC (Post Computers).

EDUCATION FOR LIVING

~~~~~~

♡ Day 15 of **SUMMER** holidays ♡

♡ 28 days to start of HIGH SCHOOL ♡

♡ 9 days after CHRISTMAS ♡

♡ 6 sleeps before AG arrives ♡

~~~~~~

SAVE ME! SOMEBODY SAVE ME!

'Life is difficult', that's what it says in one of my self-help books and I'm here to tell you, with all the catastrophic catastrophes that have catastrophised my life of late, that is an understatement.

Today is the first day in forever I've been able to face writing in my diary.

We're all at our beach shack in Poowong now. Surprisingly the holiday homes were very cheap here so Mum and Dad snapped one up for a song when I was just a baby. It could have something to do with the LEGEND OF THE POOWONG BIG HEAD.

There have been many sightings in the nearby forest of this part-human/part-animal creature with its distinctive HUGE HEAD. However only one photograph of it exists—a very grainy photo, that to me looks like a shadow more than an actual creature. Shadow or not, I have to admit it does have a big head. Of course every souvenir shop within a 20-kilometre radius has this grainy, barely decipherable image of the Poowong Big Head printed on everything from teatowels to bathers. Who in their right mind would buy bathers with the Poowong Big Head printed on them?

POOWON‹
big head

My mother apparently . . .

This will be something I raise in therapy when I'm much older.

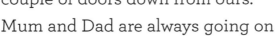

Ponky and his family are at their shack too, which is a couple of doors down from ours. Mum and Dad are always going on about how good it is to get away from it all, to which Ponky's parents always nod in agreement, 'Ahhhh yes, great to get away from it all.' I don't know if they realise that 'getting away from it all' is very similar to 'not getting away from it all', given Ponky's family are still our neighbours and we're together practically every day.

Anyway, I thought getting away from it all might make things better but no, it hasn't. Thankfully Ag arrives in 6 MORE SLEEPS! YAY! But it is with great sadness that the first order of business will be to announce . . .

OPERATION BETTER US'S IS OVER!!!

My attempts to 'change for the better' have been one big fat FAILURE and I'm not even being dramatic. In fact I'm being very un-dramatic. Let's talk Christmas for starters. Dessert was left in the hands of Grandma and she turned up with a pav. To understand the gravity of this action, we have to go back, way back...

JUST SAY 'I DO' ...

My mum and dad had been together for a long time, they'd had kids, built their dream home but had never gotten married. Then, on the 10th anniversary of their first date, Mum announced they were getting married. This was...

HUGE!

COLOSSAL!

MASSIVE!!

That's because Mum always said she didn't believe in marriage 'cos it's just another example of '**gender inequality**'. It sounded so serious I was always too scared to ask what that meant. Turns out **gender inequality** is all about the things girls **aren't allowed** to do just because **we're girls!!!** Sometimes it's been that way for so long that we girls don't even realise we're being **gender inequalitied**. Which is why Mum always said until it's completely acceptable for women to ask men to marry them, then she will continue to see marriage as just another *example* of **gender inequality**. So what changed? Turns out Mum **ASKED** Dad to marry her!!! Mum said if you want to change the world, you might as well start by changing the things *you* do.

I was the flower girl, of course, and got to wear the most beautiful ye. oldie-worldie. dressie. Leif was the ring bearer and had to wear ye. oldie-worldie. suitie. complete with KNICKERBOCKERS! I love that Mum and Dad have giant blown-up photos of us hanging in THE LOUNGE (DA-DA DA DAAAAA!). I, of course, carried off ye. oldie-worldie. look with great PIZZAZZLE.

But Leif . . . let's just say I go look at his photo whenever I need a good laugh.

LET'S GIVE IT AN AUSSIE THEME . . .

With Dad being German, Grandma got this idea in her head that the wedding needed a bit of an Aussie theme, so she made a three-tiered pav for the wedding cake. Mum was not impressed, in fact she was very unimpressed.

Three-tiered PAV

'You do realise this is my wedding and not a backyard barbecue.!'

Then Grandma got a bit uppity telling Mum that this pav was better than Gammy's! Gammy is my Great-Grandma who's over a century old and she won 1st prize for her pav sometime last century at the 'Nar Nar Goon Fair'. And YES, Nar Nar Goon is an actual town. But back to Mum who, the second she saw that pav, looked like this . . .

MUM-O-METER

Mum said she didn't want to hear another word about that pav!

Moving on . . . we were all at the church. Gammy in her wheelchair, Grandma at her side, both of them smiling . . . until it was time for Mum's vows. She told all the guests the story of how she asked Dad to marry her and they loved it! Dad stood beside her, chest out, so proud.

Grandma was definitely not proud. In fact, VERY unproud. 'OH, MARGARET! AND IN A CHURCH!' she said really loudly and everyone laughed, except Grandma, who obviously didn't find it funny at all. But Gammy, who had fallen asleep, was smiling . . . which was weird because she's always so grumpy . . . so it couldn't have been as bad as Grandma thought.

Oh, Margaret! And in a **CHURCH!**

While we were having our photos taken, Grandma lost her Nar Nar Goon at Mum . . .

At the reception, which was at this really posh place, Grandma kept telling anyone who'd listen how she constructed her amazing three-tiered pav, how it was better than Gammy's prize-winning pav and she couldn't wait till it came time to cut the cake.

Mum said it's not a cake, it's a pav and there was not to be another word about that pav!

Mum and Dad danced the Bridal Waltz and halfway through Dad did the most beautiful thing. He wheeled Gammy onto the floor and pushed her around in a dazzling wheelchair dance. It was so touching, everyone was crying. There was no denying she was having a great time 'cos you couldn't wipe that smile off her face.

We took lots of photos with Gammy because as Mum said, she hadn't seen her smile like that in years. Dad even sat on her lap and kissed her on the cheek. Normally she'd slap him away if he came anywhere near her, but not today. She was having a ball, even if she was asleep. Even Grandma had to admit this was obviously a very happy day for Gammy.

Then it came time to cut the
wedding pav and just as the
photographer was about to snap
Mum and Dad taking a bite from
each other's slices, Grandma comes
screaming through the crowd, 'Wait!
Gammy has to try it first! She'll tell

you ALL this pav is better than hers!' Grandma pushed
a giant slice towards Gammy.

Gammy didn't open wide. Gammy didn't do
anything because turns out Gammy wasn't asleep.
Gammy was DEAD!!

Quick as a flash, Dad wheeled Gammy to the kitchen, 'Everybotty, **let's partee**, yah! DJ, **pump up zee folume!**'

The DJ did . . . with the song **Stayin' Alive**.

'Change that song right **NOW!**' Mum screamed at him. So then he played **Born to Be Alive**. What was wrong with this DJ? In the end it didn't matter, everybody was dancing, even if Gammy **was** dead in the kitchen.

STAYING ALIVE

And that is why Grandma still refers to Mum and Dad's wedding as 'the day you killed my mother!' It's also why Mum swore she would **NEVER** eat Grandma's **pav** again.

R.I.P.
GAMMY

THE PAV OF DOOM RETURNS . . .

So when Grandma turned up to Christmas lunch with the PAV OF DOOM, the question everyone was too scared to ask was . . .

> In the name of
> `GREAT` AUSTRALIAN
> **DESSERTS,**
> what was Grandma
> thinking???!!

Ding! Idea moment!
I would save the day!

The new improved me, with all I'd learnt from the one-and-a-half self-help books I'd read, would not only be able to handle myself, but I'd also have this family singing JINGLE BELLS like a professional choir in no time. And if singing 'Dashing through the snow, in a one-horse open sleigh' while bushfires raged around the country is what it took to bring my family together, then I was prepared to do it.

Mum was slamming things around the kitchen but not saying anything. I'd read about this exact thing so I said, 'Mum, you are SHOWING us your feelings but you need to SPEAK your feelings.'

Well, Mum let us know EXACTLY how she felt, but I'm not allowed to say words like that . . .

Then Grandma let Mum know how she felt by throwing the pav in the rubbish bin.

'We're using our words, Grandma, remember?'

Oh, she remembered alright. Let's just say this was definitely an MA 15+ conversation but the G-rated version went something like this . . .

Mum: 'You — — how — could you? — — are you — trying to destroy our — Christmas with your — — pav?'

Grandma: ' — — — — —!'

And so for the first time ever, we had Christmas lunch in silence. I'd like to think it was out of our deep respect for the birth of baby Jesus. But it wasn't. I don't know if I aimed too high or the scars of the pav ran too deep or self-help books are a pile of poo. One thing I did know was . . .

I FAILED!

SIDE-THOUGHT: Why did Grandma bring a pav. Why? Why? END SIDE-THOUGHT

SIDE-SIDE-THOUGHT: Just because you haven't written anything lately ... I know you're reading this, Leif. END SIDE-SIDE-THOUGHT

Am not! . . . Leif did not write this.

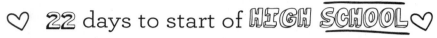
THE DUDMEISTER DON'T ROLL . . .

AG has ARRIVED!

Yay! She'd come in on the first bus, but it wasn't until we sat down for lunch that we realised she was there. I haven't worked up the courage to tell her and Ponky the news about Operation Better Us's. I don't know what I'm so worried about. They'll probably be relieved. As if they would have done any preparation anyway, what with the start of high school a mere three weeks away!!!

Not that I want to PANIC anyone!

Ag keeps asking if something is wrong. I'm going to have to come clean but I plan to do it tonight at the minigolf course, somewhere between the 9th and 18th holes.

And talking of planning, Dad has announced we'll be leaving at precisely 7.07pm, because Dad knows it takes precisely 23 minutes to walk there. Dad likes 'precisely'. He has a timetable for everything. There's no Estimated Time of Departure in our family, it's Precise Time of Departure (PTD). Estimated Time of Arrival? That would be a Precise Time of Arrival (PTA). He even has a PTD and PTA for when it's time to have fun on holidays, which kind of makes holidays the OPPOSITE OF HOLIDAYS.

You know how you're supposed to relax and roll with stuff? We don't roll. There's no rolling in our family, unless it's timetabled by the Funmeister, as Dad calls himself. No-one has the heart to tell him he's more like the Dudmeister. And tonight he's being especially obsessed with the PTD and PTA because we have to BE on time to register for The Annual Poowong Minigolf Tournament.

This is something the regular holiday-makers of Poowong see as a bit of fun ... and then there's my mum and dad. The **'Tiger Woods Twins' of minigolf.** They won't even have Leif or me on their team because when it comes to minigolf, we're not up to scratch. (Hey, their words.) This year they're set to break the record by winning a **THIRD STRAIGHT TOURNAMENT,** which is making them completely unbearable, as in 'they think they're famous' unbearable.

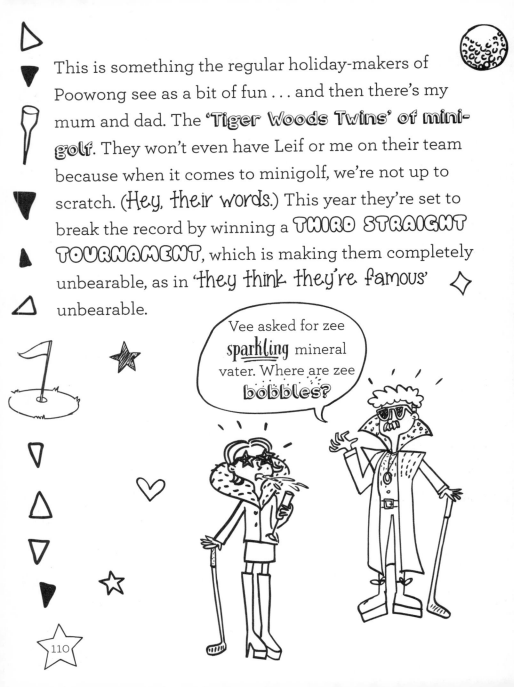

Vee asked for zee **sparkling** mineral vater. Where are zee **bobbles?**

MINIGOLF, MAJOR EMBARRASSMENT ...

Something else that's quite unbearable with this whole minigolf thing is the actual minigolf course. 'Around The World in 18 Holes', that's what it's actually called, because at every hole, miniature, crapiture replicas of world-famous attractions are plonked upon the luscious fake-green grass. Oh look, we're in the USA because there's MINI MOUNT RUSHMORE. A mini Sphinx! We must be in mini Egypt. A MINI WINDMILL ... with normal-sized clogs neatly placed outside. Quite obviously out of scale, unless a DUTCH GIANT lives there!!! And look at the mini-largest waterfall in the world ... mini Victoria Falls in mini Zambia! This place was A HOLE, all 18 OF THEM. It's embarrassing just walking through the entrance, let alone having to be part of the tournament.

That's why before tee off, Ponky and I told Ag the one and only rule she needed to know—lose. Obviously we don't want to be wasting our time playing minigolf.

Yes, we would have to be there to cheer on the 'Woods Twins', but us getting knocked out at the first round meant we'd get to hang with the other kids, grab an ice-cream and have a normal schedule-free vacation, even if it was only for a couple of hours at a time. And Mum and Dad would be left in peace with their **WINNING** obsession, which is so bad I am positively positive I could run past them **naked** with my **hair on fire** and they'd probably ask me to grab **them** some water.

ARE YOU CRAZY?

So there we were at the Mini Great Wall of China, doing an excellent job of losing I might add, when I casually dropped **the big news** about Operation Better Us's ...

'**ARE YOU CRAZY?**' Ag said. And she said it so **fearlessly** and **loudly**, like she really meant it. It was as if she was a completely different Ag. I almost asked if whoever she was, could she please return the real Ag? And Ponky said he was **really disappointed** because he'd been working on stuff. Obviously he had 'cos he'd just **expressed his feelings.** And that's when I started

Are you **CRAZY?**

CRYING.

My friends had moved forward and I was stuck. I told them everything, how I'd **failed horribly** at **changing**, how the new me ruined Christmas and unless my parents agreed to home schooling, high school was looking **hellishly hellish** for me.

'You wanna keep holding everyone up or move on?' came a voice from nowhere.

'Did you hear that?' I asked. 'That voice from nowhere? He said to move on. **It's a sign!**'

'No, it's that guy behind you,' said Ponky.

'What guy?' I said as I swung round, minigolf club on my shoulder. **THWUNK!** Oh, that guy, the one lying **facedown** on the fake grass of mini China. How could he be **SO STUPID**, something I felt the need to point out. 'YOU CAN'T STAND THAT CLOSE TO SOMEONE'S MINI CLUB AND NOT EXPECT...'

He rolled over, and apart from the bleeding gash and his now-swollen cheekbone, he could well have been **an angel**.

How, in the name of the Chinese Mongoose, are people born this **GOOD-LOOKING?** Everything beyond this moment is a bit of a blur, but Ponky and Ag told me I was babbling like an idiot, '*You're completely right*. I do need to move on and not just to **mini Canada** with the really cute **mini beavers** but with **my entire life**. You're so wise, **OH GREAT GIFT FROM THE GODS!**' Blur, blur, blur, reality kicking in at the ice-cream parlour, somewhere around the time I planted a lemon gelato cone **onto his cheek**. I *thought* the ice would prevent further swelling, while the citrus would disinfect the wound.

HA-HA HA-HA

Ag laughed so hard, choc-mint ice-cream came out her nose. In fact, everyone there laughed so hard, the whole place became one BIG

snotty mess of ice-cream.

But I didn't care. BOMD—oh, that's my codename for him, **Boy Of My Dreams**, the one I **clubbed in the head**, (I mean if anyone reads this I certainly don't want them to know who BOMD is just in case they decide to tell him how much I like him— **suffer Leif**), I just cared that he was going to be OK.

GIRL TALK . . .

That night in bed, Ag and I talked and talked and she **pointed out** something **really important**. She said my clubbing of **BOMD** showed I can change. When I whacked him, **I went straight into point 5**—not thinking before I spoke. But other than that, Ag said, there were so many things **I DID RIGHT**. I apologised, I didn't blame BOMD, didn't argue about who was right or wrong or become obsessed with having the last word. Ag was right!!! And with BOMD ending up in hospital with concussion and all, combined with the medication they have him on, there's a good chance he won't remember any of the mistakes I made. I could start afresh as . . .

TRACY LACY

the NEW improved

UPLOADED,

rebooted, reinstalled

☆ VERSION 1.1 ☆

This idea definitely had some promising promise, so while Ag lay there in her bed, I went over my list of faults and realised that everything on there came down to

four main things . . .

1. **I must 'self-censor'**. Basically, when my brain wants me to blurt something out, stop and think first.

2. **I will be a 'show-off-free-zone'**. Basically, there is no need for me to go out of my way to impress people in the hope they will like me.

3. **I shall 'un-argue'**. Basically, even if I am right, I will not **disagree, squabble, bicker** or **fight** just to prove a point.

4. **I will 'un-un-listen'**. Basically, I will listen instead of doing my own thing.

I was admiring my new super-condensed list when my brain was struck  by bolts of

ΣXCITΣ⋆NING

(like lightning but with excitement mixed in).

'What if I actually changed?' I said to Ag. 'What if BOMD ended up really, really liking TRACY LACY— THE NEW IMPROVED UPLOADED, REBOOTED, REINSTALLED, VERSION 1.1?' I said. 'Maybe me clubbing BOMD nearly to death is exactly what I needed to make this work, to make me change?' I said.

'Maybe it is!' said Ag as she walked back into the room with a glass of water. (In the name of ninjas, if Ag was coming back into the room, how long had I been talking to an empty bed?)

So BOMD was the kid taken away in the ambulance to have his cheek stitched up. Yeah, I'll never work out who that guy is.

ARRRGGHH!
STOP READING MY DIARY, OR AT THE RISK OF REPEATING MYSELF
YOU WILL BE SORRY!

Dear Homicide Squad, should you find me bludgeoned to death with a minigolf club, it was HER!

♡ Day 22 of **SUMMER** holidays ♡
♡ 21 days to start of HIGH SCHOOL ♡
♡ 1 day since I ~~clobbered~~ met BOMD ♡

MORE MINIGOLF . . .

Oh yay, another night at the minigolf. If it weren't for the hope of seeing BOMD, I would have faked illness.

♡ Day 23 of **SUMMER** holidays ♡
♡ 20 days to start of HIGH SCHOOL ♡
♡ 2 days since I met BOMD . . . ♡
♡ hopefully it didn't leave a scar ♡

AND MORE MINIGOLF . . . ☆

THEY KEEP WINNING!!! I don't know how many times they've been around THAT STUPID MINI-WORLD but I'm already mini-jet-lagged. Their desire to become the first team to take out ~~three~~ consecutive tournaments is most un-normal. Even more un-normal . . . NO BOMD!! What is going on?? WHERE IS HE? Surely he wouldn't have gone back to wherever he came from without saying goodbye, or would he? If there's no BOMD tomorrow night, I'm faking tonsillitis till the end of the tournament, maybe until the end of the holidays, maybe even for the rest of my life.

BUT THEN A MIRACLE . . .

Miraculously, A MIRACLE occurred! Not any old miracle but a 'we are on the same wavelength' miracle. During the Dudmeister's scheduled beach time, Ag and Ponky actually said they thought there were probably too many things on my list and maybe we should cut it back. So when I pulled out my new super-condensed list they nearly drowned!!! Well, they would have if we were in the water but we were lying on the shore so when they gasped in amazement, they sucked in a GOBFUL of sand. I guess you could say it was a sand drowning.

Anyway, my new list was given the . . .

OPERATION BETTER US'S

SEAL OF APPROVAL

BUT HANG ON A SEC . . .

Why were Ag and Ponky suddenly SO INTO
Operation Better Us's? Time to spit it out, not just the
sand but the truth. Turns out, with the first day of high
school a mere 17 DAYS AWAY (not that I want
to create a general panic!!!) they'd realised walking
through the high school gates in a mere 17 DAYS
(not that they wanted to create a general panic!!!)
did require some hardcore preparation, because since
hanging out with the kids at the minigolf every night,
they'd also realised they needed to lift their game.

They were not really making much progress on the **fitting-in front**. Seems someone's Operation Better Us's idea was not as completely **COO-COO BANANAS** as everyone first thought!

SIDE-THOUGHT: We needed to make this work, but how? **END SIDE-THOUGHT**

SIDE-SIDE-THOUGHT: Having read one-and-a-half self-help books, I was practically a qualified psychologist. I could make this work. **END SIDE-SIDE-THOUGHT**

SIDE-SIDE-SIDE-THOUGHT: I needed to make this work **NOW!** **END SIDE-SIDE-SIDE-THOUGHT**

And so I began . . . 'The first thing we need to do,' I said, 'is have a no-holds barred, straight-from-the-heart, heart-to-heart about what we're most afraid of.'

'Yes!' they said, PRACTICALLY JUMPING at the chance to unload their problems.

See, that's true friendship right there. We TRUST each other so much we can do that.

Ponky started. He said he's afraid of meeting all the new kids at high school, that he'll probably clam up because he always does when he feels afraid or shy or

even **angry**. Ponky said he doesn't know how to deal with this **feeling** stuff, so he just sulks.

Mmmm, seems like a **certain someone** was most certainly right when she handed her list to Ponky. (**Hint**: It wasn't Ag.) Not that being right is important, even if you are right **MOST** of the time. (Apparently, this can offend people so just forget I mentioned it.)

Anyway . . . then Ag shared her fears and said she was afraid **everyone** would think she was a **WEIRDO** because, for some strange reason, people get a **big fright** when she says simple things like 'Hi'. (Er . . . yes, ninja girl.)

She wants to fit in, not **superstar, ultra-popular-status** fit in, just not be **weirdo-ninja-girl.** (She didn't actually say 'weirdo-ninja-girl' but I think it best describes what she did say.) AND . . . I do believe this was **EXACTLY** what I wrote on the list I gave to Ag. But me being right is not what's important here, so moving on . . .

My turn . . . I think we all knew what I was going to say before I said it. I was afraid of becoming the **completely coo-coo bananas girl AGAIN** and I was willing to do whatever it took to make sure it **never, ever** happened **AGAIN** . . . starting with taking back all that stuff I just wrote about being right.

'The time has come to tackle our fears head on,' I said. 'If we have any hope of our former polka-dancing selves surviving high school, now is the time to act.'

'But how?' Ponky asked. Eek, I'd sounded so convincingly convincing but I think I may have been a little unprepared with my convincingness. Long silence . . . that quickly turned awkward because Ag and Ponky were staring at me like I had the answer. Argh! The pressure! Tick, tock, tick, tock . . . DING!

IDEA MOMENT!

And my ideas spewed forth like molten magma from an erupting volcano!

I'm sure I could hear grand, inspirational music blaring for all to hear as I stood tall upon a small mound of sand giving my 'sermon from the mound' . . .

'Friends, we need do only one thing. That thing?

THE OPPOSITE OF WHAT WE WOULD NORMALLY DO!

Ponky, when you don't want to express your feelings . . . you express.

YOU DIG DEEP AND EXPRESS FOR ALL TO HEAR.

Ag, you make yourself noticed from the second you walk into a room and you own that room like

YOU'RE THE MAYOR OF THIS TOWN WE LOVINGLY KNOW AS POOWONG!

Me, I "un-coo-coo-bananas" myself by following

MY NEW SUPER-CONDENSED LIST.

And we start now! And we work hard! And we become better people!

And my friends, being in Poowong is our **SAVING GRACE** because if we fail, we don't have to see any of these kids 320 days a year for the next six years of our lives.

Be **UNAFRAID OF FAILURE** but embrace trying and let's get out there and give it our best shot!

OBULOG IS GO!'

INSPIRED BY MY WORDS, Ag and Ponky applauded loudly . . . well that's what I expected they'd do, but no . . . nothing but silence . . .

'Operation Better Us's—Lift Our Game?' I clarified.

More silence . . .

OBULOG!
That stands for
OBULOG!

Now awkard silence, which I was tempted to fill when suddenly Ag and Ponky jumped to their feet, JUMPING FOR JOY. (No, they really did!)

It's brilliant!

It's so simple!

'Where's our stuff?' I said.

Well on its way to Vanuatu by the looks of it.

We'd been so **ENGROSSED** in our sharing and caring, solutions and deliberations, we didn't notice it had been washed away.

Oh well, a small price to pay for our social survival.

Not that Mum saw it that way.

MUM-O-METER

OBULOG . . .

That night, as usual, we all headed off to the minigolf. Me, Ag and Ponky were almost power-walking, we were so keen to get there and put OBULOG into action. Mum and Dad and Ponky's parents thought it was so sweet that we were so keen to cheer on Mum and Dad. But Leif could smell a rat, I could tell by his 'I know you're up to something' smirk.

I know you're up to something SMIRK

Mum and Dad walked onto the green to the cheers of the Poowong crowd. They actually took a bow. Oh, this was beyond embarrassing.

CHEER! YAY! WOO-HOO! HOORAY!

We gave an obligatory 'YAY TEAM!' before making a beeline for the ice-cream parlour. We were one step inside the door when suddenly Ag announced, 'Hi everyone, my name's Ag, nice to meet you all.' Then she made her way to the counter, shaking everyone's hands, greeting them as if she were THE MAYOR!

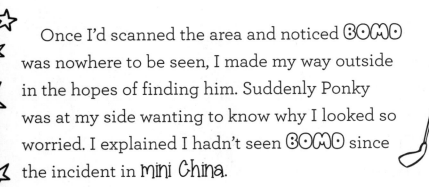

At least she'd been listening to my OBULOG speech and at least she was no longer 'weirdo-ninja-girl' just 'different-weirdo-ninja-girl'.

Once I'd scanned the area and noticed BOMO was nowhere to be seen, I made my way outside in the hopes of finding him. Suddenly Ponky was at my side wanting to know why I looked so worried. I explained I hadn't seen BOMO since the incident in mini China.

What if he was still in hospital, in a coma, on life support, hanging on by a thread?

'We've got to go see if he's OK,' Ag said, scaring **the bejingo** out of us. Yes, she'd been there the whole time. **Weirdo-ninja-girl** was back, but like we agreed, this wasn't about success it was about trying.

To the hospital!

It would have been such a **superhero exit** if Leif hadn't been blocking our path.

'We'll be back by the time they're in mini Brazil so go for your life.' Leif was stunned that I had actually stood up to him, but then so was I. I didn't care if he had to scale the summit of mini Mount Everest to tell on me, I HAD TO FIND BOMO!

WE'VE COME TO HELP THE DYING . . .

We were at the reception desk of the hospital when I realised I didn't know BOMO's name. None of us did! The receptionist asked how she could help. Thinking **fast** and **desperate** to find BOMO I just started talking . . .

'We are members of a special group of young people who visit hospitals to **help the dying**. We spend time talking to them about their fears of passing over to the other side. We offer **company**, grab them their **last cup of tea** before they walk into the light, that kind of thing. Do you have anyone here **dying, comatose or on life support** who might like a cup of tea?'

She stared at us like we were nuts.

'More specifically, do you have a teenage boy here who may or may not have suffered a life-threatening knock to the head? Very good-looking? Gash to the cheek? Ringing any bells?'

Ringing any bells?

RECEPTION

GET OUT!

Here we were, offering help for the sick and dying and she says 'get out' and with a tone of such ingratitude.

'Well, excuse us for caring!' I said but Ag and Ponky were already dragging me out, whispering 'OBULOG, Tracy! OBULOG!' Darn, I'd completely let my concern for BOMO take over.

Well, EXCUSE us for caring!

★ SIDE-THOUGHT: In times of stress beware. Ensure OBULOG is at forefront of mind. END SIDE-THOUGHT ★

SIDE-SIDE-THOUGHT: Maybe it was time I faced facts, BOMO had gone home ... or died. END SIDE-SIDE-THOUGHT

DEUM . . .

'**DEUM!**' Ponky suddenly shouted bringing us to an **immediate** halt. '**What the heck** is going on with this whole **BOMO** thing?' he demanded.

Astonished by his **astonishing astonishment**, I told him, 'Nothing.'

'AHHHHHH!' Ag gasped. 'You want him to be your **boyfriend**!'

See, this is the problem with having such close friends. They know you too well. There was no use denying what Ag had said. I fessed up, 'OK, yes, I thought if I practised my OBULOG on BOMO and he liked me then I could see that it **really was working** and that I had changed.'

Ponky said that didn't make sense because BOMO has never met the *real* Tracy Lacy so he can't compare her with OBULOG TRACY LACY.

I said I disagreed. No boy has ever *really* liked me, they all run a mile so if BOMO liked me then that would mean OBULOG had worked.

Ponky went **all sulky** but then he announced, 'I am now going to EXPRESS MY FEELINGS on this because I think I am experiencing some.'

WOW! This was progress!

'Excuse me for being a **boy** who **likes you**, and as I have said since we were little, will one day **marry you** . . .'

SIDE-THOUGHT: In the name of the BRIDAL WALTZ, when will Ponky realise no-one finds his declarations of marriage cute or funny anymore? **END SIDE-THOUGHT**

'. . . but maybe you should take **BOMO**'s disappearance as a **SIGN**.'

'A sign of what?' I asked.

That YOU are TOO YOUNG to have a BOYFRIEND!

WELL, I thought, Ponky seemed to have latched onto this concept of *expressing his feelings in record time!* Of course I wanted to tell him with **absolute absoluteness** that he was absolutely wrong, but I had to think of **OBULOG** AND the ever-so-slight problem that I had no idea what it meant to have a boyfriend when you're 12. I had to actually admit I didn't know something. This too was progress.

'Ag, Ponky,' I said, 'I have no idea what having a boyfriend actually means.' But they said they didn't either so we discussed it the entire walk back. And I have to admit . . . **WE ARE GENIUSES!** I couldn't wait to write all our **genius** thoughts into my diary. The questions we answered were the kind of questionable questions they should put in a self-help book . . .

Does having a boyfriend/girlfriend mean you have to hold hands?

No, because you don't want anyone to know you have a boyfriend or girlfriend, **especially** the boyfriend or girlfriend.

Do you have to kiss them?

ABSOLUTELY NOT, that would be gross. No kissing!

Do you have to hang out with your boyfriend or girlfriend?

Yes, but only in large groups, **never** alone because that would be too awkward.

Do you have to tell your boyfriend/girlfriend you like them?

No way! You don't want your boyfriend or girlfriend to know you actually **LIKE** them.

So what does having a boyfriend or girlfriend actually mean?

It means that a boyfriend or girlfriend is more of a **concept relationship** than a **relationship relationship**.

Everything was **crystal clear** to me now ... I was **deeply** in concept love with **BOMO** and **desperately** wanted him to be my **concept boyfriend**. But given he was 'no longer with us' I guess it didn't matter anymore. At least I was **prepared** if ever I fell in concept love again.

We arrived back just in time to see Mum and Dad win their round. Oh yay, would this never end? Leif eyeballed me from across the crowd, giving me the 'I'm watching you' signal like he was some kind of super spy. He's gathering intelligence to use against me, I just know it.

Oh, the things I know. You should be worried dear sister, because when you least expect it, BAM! The Leifmeister will be there to do something with the stuff he knows.

Shut up, Leif. And since when have you started referring to yourself in the third person?

The Leifmeister doesn't even know what that means.

Tracy thinks it's time you worked it out.

♡ ♡ Day **28** of **SUMMER** holidays
♡ **15** days to start of HIGH SCHOOL ♡
♡ **7** days since I saw BOMD—what, he's ♡
♡ in the witness-protection program now? ♡

VEE A TEAMS, YAH! . . .

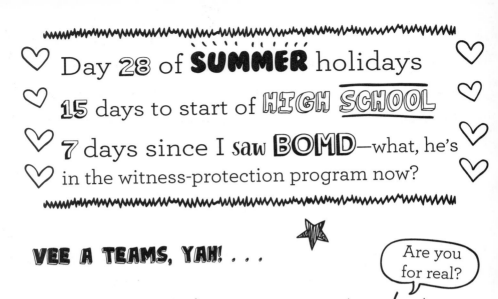

'Are you for real?' Yes, my brother Leif, the GOLDEN CHILD, the one who does no wrong, actually said those words to Mum and Dad. Why? Well, like all of us he was shocked at the shocking shock of bright-yellow T-shirts, complete with Team Lacy, Here To Kick Up A Storm printed in big, bold letters across the front. This was a slogan that would make no sense to anyone unless you know my parents have different surnames, which most of Poowong doesn't.

148

A moment to explain more fully . . . yes, my dad's surname is Storm, my mum's is Lacy. Mum's **gender inequality** theory with surnames is that the woman's surname is just as acceptable as the man's. And she's right. I just sometimes wonder why she chose Tracy as my first name. But back to the T-shirts . . .

'I don't see zee proplem! Vee haff made **zee qvawter finals** tomorrow, you shoult be **prout** to vear zem. Vee a teams, yah!'

Oh boy, where do I begin? *Yes, dear parents, we love that our **entire holiday** has been hijacked by your obsession with MINIGOLF. And we're ESPECIALLY EXCITED at having TO WEAR bright-yellow T-shirts so that we can be TEASED AND LAUGHED AT.*

That's what I **wanted** to say but I didn't (I think this was progress). But when everyone else started protesting, I could no longer hold my tongue . . . (I think I just went back to un-progress).

Dad's eyes started going all red and teary. He said it was his **cat allergy** ... but we don't have a cat. The yellow T-shirts stayed. Dad's cat allergy disappeared.

Day 29 of **SUMMER** holidays

14 days to start of HIGH SCHOOL

8 days since I saw **BOMD**—he's but a memory—or did I mortally wound him?

KEEPING UP WITH THE . . .

With all the camera flashes, you could have sworn we were one of those famous families on television that are famous for being a family on television. The *Poowong Times* were there snapping photos of us in our yellow T-shirts. Great, I'm going to be on the front page of the local paper looking like a giant canary.

As usual, Ag, Ponky and I gave the required '**GO TEAM!**' then turned to disappear only . . .

I TURNED STRAIGHT INTO **BOMD!**

It was him, right there, in front of me, centimetres away. I was so **flustered** and **excited** my brain didn't know whether to say 'hi' or 'hello' so what came out was 'hi-lo'.

HI-LO?!??!!

OK, maybe he didn't notice, just please don't notice the T-shirt, please don't notice the T-shirt.

'Hi-lo to you. Nice T-shirt.'

Great! It's OK, Tracy. Let it go, laugh it off.

'HA HA HA HA HA HA! AHHHH! HA HA HA HA!'

Hi-lo to you. Nice T-shirt

TEAM LACY here STORM A STORM

152

It wasn't THAT funny, why was I laughing like he was the hilarious good-looking guy in a sitcom?

'My mum and dad dressed me.'

Numbats! That's definitely not what I meant to say.

Seeing my struggle, Ag and Ponky jumped in to save me, suggesting we all head to the ice-cream joint. Sometimes I think my friends know me better than I know myself. On the way there, I pulled myself together, brain working overtime . . .

OBULOG!

1. Self-censor.
2. Be a 'show-off-free zone'.
3. Un-argue.
4. Un-un-listen.

That's all I had to do and probably steer clear from entering the parlour, given I could be mistaken for a giant banana ice-cream.

So there I was outside waiting for Ag and Ponky while they got their ice-creams. Ag was caught up introducing herself to everyone as part of her un-ninja plan. I was reminding myself to talk to her about alternate ways to execute her plan when suddenly . . .

BOMO WAS AT MY SIDE!!!

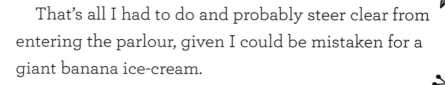

No, this was awkward, way too awkward. I waved to Ag and Ponky, signalling for them to come join/rescue me but they just waved back. What happened to those friends who knew me better than I knew myself? Could they not see this was a 'rescue me' wave not a 'hey, how you doing?' wave? But then BOMO started talking and everything became a bit easier because he liked to talk . . . a lot. No really, not just a lot, but A LOT!!! All I really remember is . . .

BOMO: Talk, talk, talk, talk, talk, talk, talk, talk, talk, talk, talk, talk, talk, talk, talk, **I really like football**.

I really wanted to say 'That's so weird, I really like ballet.' But I was 1. Self-censoring so ...

ME: Great.

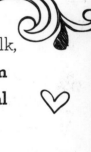

BOMO: Talk, talk, talk, talk, talk, talk, talk, talk, talk, talk, talk, talk, talk, talk, talk, talk, talk, talk, **I'm really good at it so I'm going to be a professional footy player** ...

I wanted to tell him 'I'm really good at ballet and I want to dance professionally' but 2. Show-off-free zone so ...

ME: Fantastic.

BOMO: Talk, talk, talk, talk, talk, talk, talk, talk, talk, talk, talk, talk, talk, talk, talk, talk, **did you know footy players are the fittest people in the world?**

Oh, this was completely wrong because I happened to know the results of a recent test that proved dancers to be fitter than any other athlete. True fact. But, 3. Un-argue . . .

ME: Maybe. (I couldn't quite let it go. I thought 'maybe' was a good compromise.)

BOMO: I have to go. See ya.

SEE YA? SEE YA?!!?

I threw my face into my pillow crying and yelling at the same time, 'Peehell ay oo-i oo air ets ee ore enooiasm.'

'Are you speaking in Latin, because if you are, I'm very impressed,' Ponky said trying to comfort me.

'I said ... PEOPLE SAY GOODBYE TO THEIR PETS WITH MORE ENTHUSIASM! JUST SAY IT, PONKY, I ACTED LIKE A COMPLETE TWIT!'

'Well, I wasn't there so I can't really say.'

'Three words, Ponky, **three!** "Great", "fantastic" and "maybe". No wonder he had to go! He needed to get to the nearest hospital 'cos of his **NEAR-FATAL CASE OF BOREDOM!**'

'Well, I like you just the way you are,' Ponky said. 'And one day when we're married, you'll see that.'

'Can I be your Maid of Honour?' **BAM!** Our heads hit the bunks. In the name of the bejingo-jingoes, Ag had been there the whole time!

SIDE-THOUGHT: Research Ag's surname. Find out if Smith is of Japanese origin. **END SIDE-THOUGHT**

Ag suggested maybe I'd taken OBULOG too seriously. 'The whole idea is to make us better people—not boring people,' she said and she was right. But for me it looked like a lose/lose situation. Either I stay completely coo-coo bananas and high school is just like primary school, only worse, OR, I change and become the completely boring-boring-bananas girl. I needed time to re-evaluate and to recover from this life-threatening case of humiliation. There was no way I was going near that minigolf course tomorrow. Seeing BOMO would be the most humiliating humiliation of all time.

HO HUM. Completely **BORING- BORING- BANANAS** girl

(ME)

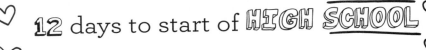

Day **31** of **SUMMER** holidays

12 days to start of **HIGH SCHOOL**

2 days since I *epically* stuffed up being a *normal human being* in front of **BOMD**, gah!

TONSILLITIS SCHMONSILLITIS . . .

Before Mum and Dad left for their semi-final match, they gave me a big kiss and cuddle and told Ag to make sure she looked after me. 'I'ne oh 'orry I 'an't 'ake it. 'Ood 'uck.' It was A BRILLIANT ... 'I'll-be-lucky-to-last-the-night-with-this-tonsillitis' PERFORMANCE.

Unfortunately, Ponky's parents decided, with two of the cheer squad at home, Ponky would have to throw on the team shirt and cheer **twice as loud**. We felt **awful** seeing Ponky in his yellow T-shirt being dragged out, looking back at us with his **sad little face**, the door closing, closing, closed . . .

I jumped out of bed . . . **GIRLS NIGHT IN WAS GO!** Lollies, chips, movie! Now **this** was a holiday. We were having **so much fun** when suddenly . . . well, I say suddenly but actually two hours had passed . . . Ponky burst through the door huffing and puffing like he'd run a marathon.

WHAT ???!!!!!

'**BOMO**,' puff, pant. '**LEIF**,' puff, pant. '**TALKING** . . . to each other!'

I was out of that bed faster than you could say, 'What dastardly plan is my brother up to in his attempt to torment me and destroy my entire life whilst simultaneously sending me crazy because that's . . .' Oh, look at that, I was well and truly out of bed already pacing in circles and I hadn't even finished my 'faster than you could say' saying.

'This is **bad**,' I said. '**Really bad**. I know he knows I like **BOMO**, so the worst thing he could do is . . .'

'Tell **BOMO** how **MUCH YOU LIKE HIM**!' Leif laughed as he poked his head into my room. 'Tracy and **BOMO** sitting in a tree, **K.I.S.S.I.N.G!**'

Maybe it was **THAT STUPID** rhyme that pushed me over **the edge**, maybe it was Leif's mere **existence**, the years of putting up with his **lies, tricks** and **dobbing**. Whatever it was, I had reached my limit . . .

'WHY DO YOU RUIN EVERYTHING FOR ME? YOU MAKE MY LIFE SO HARD, LEIF. ALL I WANT IS A BROTHER I CAN TRUST AND KEEP SECRETS WITH AND . . . hi Mum, hi Dad, did you win?'

MUM-O-METER

Mum and Dad didn't say anything, they just turned and walked away. I have this theory . . . when your parents yell at you, obviously you're in trouble, but when your parents say nothing, that's **trouble plus bitter disappointment**, which is **WAY, WAY, WAY WORSE**. Even Ponky's parents shook their heads as they left. I glanced at Leif expecting to see his **SMARMY, VICTORIOUS SMIRK** but strangely he kept his head down and left my room without saying another word.

LIGHTS OUT . . .

Everyone was in bed. Strangely the darkness seemed darker than usual. There were no celebrations tonight even though Mum and Dad won a place in the Poowong Minigolf Grand Final. Everyone went to bed—sad, angry, disappointed, but there was definitely no happy.

And it's ALL **MY** FAULT

BOMD says he likes you too. He said most girls just talk about themselves, but you didn't. He wants to meet up at the Minigolf Grand Final.

And . . .

I'm sorry.

Thanks! Tracy x

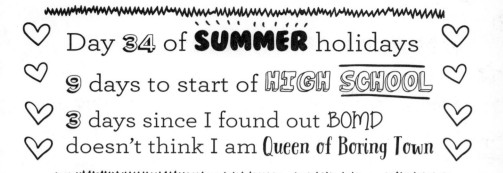

Day 34 of **SUMMER** holidays

9 days to start of HIGH SCHOOL

3 days since I found out BOMD

doesn't think I am Queen of Boring Town

HE LIKES ME! . . .

He actually likes me! Great, fantastic and maybe is all it takes to make a boy like me?!!? Every couple has their special song but BOMD and I, we had our SPECIAL WORDS—great, fantastic and maybe. Huh, no wonder boys would run a mile when they saw me coming. I'd actually tried to converse with them and be interesting and funny, when all it took was great, fantastic and maybe. Thanks to OBULOG, all is looking very promising on the concept boyfriend front. Imagine if he concept loved me! Eeeeeeee! I couldn't wait to get to the minigolf Grand Final tonight! Talking of which . . . my parents. I had to make things right which meant . . .

APOLOGISING!

SORRY SEEMS TO BE THE HARDEST WORD . . .

I've never found saying sorry easy. I know there are
times when I should say it but I don't and I'm pretty
sure that's why I insist I'm right, even when I know I'm
wrong, 'cos that way I can just be right and not have
to apologise. Truth is, I don't even know how to say
sorry. When I've tried, I just end up crying and feeling
really afraid. To put it simply . . .

 Mistake **+** Feeling **BAD** **+** Apology **✗**  **CRYING** **−**

 **FEAR** of looking like a **CRY BABY** **≡** **BETTER** to **NOT** apologise

BUT ... there was no getting around this one. I had done wrong and I felt really bad. I owed my parents an apology. They are my parents and they love me so I shouldn't be afraid, right? But I was. I had to get to the bottom of this, not just for the sake of repairing my relationship with Mum and Dad, but because I had a feeling this might help me with my OBULOG.

I consulted one of my self-help books. Eesh! Who knew saying sorry was so complicated. There were entire chapters devoted to this very topic. There's right ways to apologise, wrong ways, feelings you should feel, feelings you shouldn't, things you should say, things you shouldn't. It was a can of worms I wish I hadn't opened. And one of those worms got me thinking about Grandma and the Christmas pav. I got straight on the phone ...

'Grandma,' I said, 'why did you bring that pav to Christmas lunch?' And you know what she said? She said she was trying to say sorry. I knew it! She felt bad and this was her way of trying to move on, trying to say, 'I made a mistake, let's eat pav and love it and each other at the same time'. Unfortunately, this was on the wrong way to apologise list. But, I took comfort in the fact that I'm not the only one who finds it hard to say sorry, and bonus ... I solved the great pav mystery of Christmas lunch.

I WAS TRYING TO SAY SORRY

And so the apology to my parents was a teary affair. Dad took first prize in the tissue stakes by a good half a box. I didn't care how much I cried because I now knew this meant I felt true remorse ... and I did. Lying to them and pretending I was sick was all about me putting my stupid social life first. Knowing how much this tournament means to Mum and Dad, it made me

really sorry for what I'd done. Well! Who knew saying sorry would make you feel **SO GOOD**.

My parents **hugged me and hugged me** until I couldn't breathe. My mum, as we know, is not one for great shows of emotion but even she shed a tear, saying how **proud** she was and how **grown-up** I'd been. Dad said what I'm sure were some really loving and beautiful things, but who could understand a word of it with all that crying?

I also told them about Grandma and why she brought the **pav** to Christmas lunch. Mum took a deep breath. Obviously the scars of The Pav of Doom still ran deep. Anyway, I guess the most important thing was that I was forgiven.

WHAT MAKES A DATE 'A DATE'?

There I was alone in my room, trying on all manner of different outfits in the hope of finding the perfect look for my first date with **BOMO** when from beneath my pile of discarded clothes, Ag popped up, scaring the **bejingo-jing** out of me. (In the name of ninjas, this girl needs to be de-programmed by a ninja master!)

Once my heart rate **returned to normal**, we got straight to the business of discussing the importance of the appropriate look for a **first date**. It's a **delicate balance**—you don't want to look like you've gone to **any trouble**, but you have to go to **a lot of trouble** to look like you've not gone to any trouble. It's **VERY TROUBLESOME**. ◎

Even more troubling was Ponky arriving on the scene throwing armfuls of yellow things on my bed. **Team Lacy, Here To Kick Up a Storm** had gone **BERSERK** with the merchandising for the grand final and their chance to be the first couple to win the tournament three times in . . . blah-blah, we all know how it goes. Anyway, merchandising . . . we're talking yellow sun visors, yellow giant foam pointy finger thingys, yellow clappy thingys, yellow wizard hats. With all that yellow it looked like Big Bird had come into my room, **crapped on my bed** and left. It also looked like the **delicate balance** of appearing to have not gone to any trouble for my date had swung from **delicate** to **I've always wanted to look like a giant muppet.** Sadly, the fake tonsillitis incident left me with no bargaining power. I just hoped **BOMO** would understand my allegiance to my mum and dad had overridden any hopes for a perfect first-date outfit.

'**DATE?**' Ponky laughed. 'This is not a date.'

WHAT. DID. HE. JUST. SAY?

Ponky claimed BOMO asking me to 'meet up' at the minigolf tournament through my brother **did not** meet the criteria for a proper date. Brain goes into overdrive.

I was suddenly filled with doubt. Was my date with BOMO a real date? There was only one way to sort this out—the list challenge. Ponky versus me and Ag on what makes a date 'a date'. Pens out, paper at the ready. It was on! Moments later, BAM! We slammed our lists down ready for the debate that was to follow.

What MAKES a Date "A DATE" - TRACY and AG.

① ASKING. Basically a girl can ask a guy, a guy can ask a girl or a guy can ask a guy. A friend of a friend's friend can ask. Doesn't matter <u>who</u> asks, <u>it's a DATE</u>.

② Provided the words 'do you want to...' are followed by 'meet up', 'come to', 'go to', or any other similar phrase, <u>it's a DATE</u>.

③ If the people going on the date don't want to tell anyone, including each other, that they are going on a date, <u>it's still a DATE</u>.
      YES, concept dates <u>are allowed</u>.

④ A date can take place anywhere - parties, public events, mini golf championships, etc. provided <u>any</u> or <u>all</u> of points 1, 2, 3 and 4 have occurred.

What makes a date "A DATE" - Ponky

① The 'dater' MUST ask the 'datee' on a date face to face.

② The 'datee' must be asked formally by the 'dater' as in "Would you like to be my date for (insert event)?"

③ The dater must pick up the datee up at their home and not meet somewhere.

④ The dater MUST meet the datee's parents.

As soon as I had read Ponky's list, a very loud **'Nnnuuunnngh'** snuck out my nose and Ponky's face went straight into **sulky-puss** mode.

'Oh, come on, Ponky, seriously. Are you for real?'

'Am I for real?
Are you two for real?'
he practically growled.

Oh, come on, **PONKY**, **seriously.** Are you for **REAL?**

Uh-oh, we were again about to enter the unchartered waters of Ponky **expressing his feelings,** I was expecting it to go a bit *Titanic*/iceberg in that it was about to become another **tragic tragedy** firmly etched in the history books as one of the great disasters of our time. Our **ABSURDULOUS** conversation went like this ... and yes, I do remember it word for word ...

Me: Are you living in the **1800s**?

Ponky: Are you living in a **dream?**

AG: Come on, your list sounds like you're asking for a **girl's hand in marriage.**

Ponky: Your list sounds like you're living in **the land of 'do as you please'.**

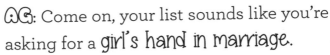

Me: We would like to be living in the land of 'do as you please', but **unfortunately** for girls it's not like that and the only way it's going to change is if we take things into our **own hands and change them.**

Ponky: That's not true! Girls can do **anything** they want, just like boys!

Me: OH REALLY???!!! According to you we're

176

supposed to wait around for Prince Charming to ask us on a date, seek our parents' approval of said date, and if we're lucky they'll let us go to the library and read books together!

AG: AND SORRY, BUT THAT'S NOT A FAIRYTALE WE WANT TO LIVE!

Me: AND IF IT WERE THE OTHER WAY AROUND, HOW WOULD YOU LIKE IT? Not that I am trying to have the last word on this, I just thought it was a valid point. Ag, please say something so you have the last word.

AG: What kind of word would you like?

Me: Any word. **Great holey cheeses.** I've done it again!

AG: Don't worry. I forgive you.

Me: Thanks, Ag. Oh, in the name of the *Oxford Dictionary*, why can't I stop saying the last word? I've stopped, OK?

AG: OK.

Me: Thank you! At last, the last word from . . . somebody tape my mouth shut right now!

'You're right,' Ponky said.

'Beg pardon?' we said, finding ourselves in such a state of shock we had to sit down.

'You're right. I wouldn't like it to be the other way around. Your list is very future-thinking and you girls are smart and brave to be changing the way people think.'

'Well, my mum said if you want to change the world, you start with you.' Thus it was settled . . . even though I had to go dressed as Big Bird's poo, I was officially going on a date with BOMO. And bonus, Ponky expressing his feelings wasn't so *Titanic*/iceberg after all.

OFF TO MY BIG DATE!
ER, MINIGOLF GRAND FINAL . . .

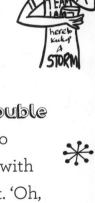

I was careful not to let on that 60% (OK 80%) of my excitement was because of my date with BOMO. The remaining 40% (but really 20%) was for my parents, who were favourites to win and become the first blah, blah, blah, etc, etc. Given I was decked out in head-to-toe yellow, I had to do something to make myself appear special, without looking like I'd gone to the trouble of looking special. Before we left, I snuck into Mum's cosmetic drawer and smothered my face with this special face cream she's always raving about. 'Oh, how it makes my skin glow. I look so fresh,' she always says. It made my skin tingle so I figured it must be doing its fresh, glowing thing already. Team Lacy, Here To Kick Up A Storm was ready!

THE SEA OF YELLOW . . .

We were crammed into 'Around the World in 18 Holes' like **sardines.** How could this many people be excited about a minigolf final? Do these people not have **lives?**

It was a sea of yellow . . . and not because every single person was supporting Mum and Dad, but it turns out their competitors had also chosen yellow as their team colour. Who'd have thunk it?

Mum and Dad were performing their warm-up routine, something they had actually worked out and practised, like they were comedians or something.

Mum starts off by saying. 'I say, Wolf, have you seen my tee?'

'Vhite viss two sugars?' Dad says as he hands Mum a cup of tea.

'No sugar and it's bright red,' Mum says as she pulls a golf tee from her pocket.

'I am such zee Dodo bird!' Dad says slapping his forehead.

'I think you mean Dodo BIIIIIRRRRRDIE!' Mum says.

And people actually laughed. No, I don't know why either.

The other finalists—**The Bobsy Twins**, 15-year-old boys, red hair, freckles—were obviously **petrified** and **COMPLETELY PSYCHED OUT** by Mum and Dad's comedy warm-up. The boys' team slogan was—**THE BOBSY TWINNERS ARE WINNERS.**

Dad turned to the spectators, 'Zee Bobsy Tvinners are Vinners? I don't sink zair English are OK.' Well, the crowd **roared with laughter** and Dad **lapped it up.** Sadly, he thought they were laughing **with** him, not **at** him.

I felt sorry for the Twins. No doubt this minigolf experience will drive them to seek therapy in years to come. We'll probably run into each other in the waiting room.

ANYONE FOR TEE OFF?

As soon as Mum and Dad teed off, we took off! Well, I turned to take off with Ag and Ponky, but they were nowhere to be seen. And among all the yellow, it's not like they were going to stand out. I pushed my way through the army of spectators towards the ice-cream parlour. With the heaving crowd, who all seemed to be staring at my face (obviously the magic face cream had worked its magic) I was worried I would end up flattened and crushed to death. Oh no, BOMO would be left heartbroken, weeping over my paper-thin, two-dimensional body. Maybe he'd have the good sense to fold me into a paper plane and keep me at his bedside, a memento of what might have been.

My face was beginning to feel really **hot** and **sticky**, but not nearly as sticky as the giant gut I turned into and bounced off. **UGH**, a man with no shirt! Actually he was wearing a shirt, **a hair-shirt!** **Oh, the humanity.** Sticky, sweaty matted gut hair sticking to my glowing skin. And the hair on his chest! It was so long he could have weaved it into a tie. **Bleurgh!**

`OH, THE HUMANITY

Suddenly I bounced into Leif, which actually pleased me after my previous bouncing experience. 'What's wrong with your face? **It's all puffy!**' he said.

'**What? Where?**' It took me a moment but then... 'Oh, I get it. You're trying to trick me into thinking I look really awful before my big date, but it's not going to work!' That showed him, I thought as I stomped away, but no, he tried it on again!

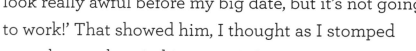

'Seriously it's **like a balloon.**'

WHATEVER!'

Just then, I spotted Ag and Ponky outside the ice-cream shop, which actually wasn't that far away, but with this crowd, it would probably take less time to trek through the Amazon. They waved at me with their giant foam hands. Oddly they seemed to be signalling **STOP! GO BACK!** But I could make out **BOMO**'s head just behind them. I cut my way through the Amazonian jungle of people with the **precision of a machete,** when Ponky thrust himself through all those people, landing at my feet.

'**You can't do this, you can't see him!**' he said. '**You have to go home!**'

WHAT?

'I thought we'd sorted this out, Ponky. Like it or not, **I have a date!**' Though I had to admit, my nerves were getting the better of me. I was burning up! I wiped the sweat from my face . . .

'You must not let him see you,' came a whisper in my ear, scaring the **bejingo-bejingy** out of me. Guess who?

'What is going on, Ag?'

'We were going to ask you the same thing,' Ag said sounding very panicky. 'It's about your fa—'

'Yo, Tracy Lacy!' It was **BOMO!!** I whirled to face him, my **concept date** standing there in all his **concept glory.** I was smiling so much my face felt like it was going to split in two.

'**WHOA!** WHAT HAPPENED TO YOUR FACE?'

I was waiting for the next sentence, which I expected would go along the lines of, 'It's so fresh and glowing.' But when it didn't come, I filled the dead air with . . .

'Oh it's just my naturally glowing skin.'

He didn't seem impressed, in fact he seemed very unimpressed, as in backing away unimpressed. It was then that I caught a glimpse of a girl in the ice-cream parlour window.

'You think I've got problems. That girl there looks like a sunburnt pufferfish.' And weirdly, she was copying everything I did. I pulled a few wacky faces which she mimicked perfectly. 'Huh, she might have the head of a giant baked bean but she's a very talented mime.' And that's when I realised the sunburnt pufferfish with the giant baked-bean head was me!

 AAAAAAAAAA RRRRRRRR-GGGGGG GGHHHHHHH!

 AAAAAAAAAA RRRRRRRRR-GGGGGG GGHHHHHHH!

And one more time just to be sure the reflection I was looking at was mine...

 AAAAAAAAAA RRRRRRRRR-GGGGGG GGHHHHHHH!

Yep, definitely me.

'We tried to tell you!' I heard Ag shouting as I ran off. Of course they did but I was too busy un-listening!!! **WOULD I EVER LEARN?**

SEE TRACY RUN . . . AGAIN!

I could feel my face **THROBBING** now. That stupid cream! Pff, makes your skin glow—yeah, like a giant full moon! Too crowded, so crowded! I leapt on some guy's shoulders and crowd-surfed my way towards the minigolf course. This did require some skill, mostly in bossiness. 'Go left, left!' I directed as the crowd joined in, carrying me above their heads. 'OK, straight ahead! **STRAIGHT AHEAD!** What's with this zig-zag bizzo? Take a right!' They went left. 'A right-right, not a left-right! Jeez, does anyone here know left from right?'

At which point **THUD!** I hit the dirt. Don't know that my last comment was appreciated.

I could feel my skin tightening over the orb that was my head. Through the slits I now had for eyes, I could see I was standing somewhere at the perimeter of the course. 'Mum! Dad! Help me!' No answer. 'Muuuuuuum!' I shouted.

From somewhere not too far away, 'Not now, darling, Dad's about to birdie at the Eiffel Tower.'

I engaged my other senses to guide me towards her voice, walking straight into the mini Swiss Alps. They collapsed around me in an avalanche of plaster. I stumbled to my feet, covered in white powder and promptly fell into the mini swamps of New Orleans. The swampy, green water, mixed with the gooey, white powder made long strands of green sludge hang from every part of my body and boy, did it stink!

I wrenched myself upright once more. '**GAAAARRRGGGHHH!**' I spluttered trying to get the stinky goop out of my mouth.

Suddenly I heard people screaming. Though virtually blind, I was desperate to know what was so terrifyingly terrible that it was terrifying everyone so terribly. '**PLAGH! PLAGH!**' I gagged trying to get the moss out of my mouth. More terrified screams.

It's the **POOWONG** BIG HEAD!! someone yelled.

'WHAAAAAAT? WHERE?' I bellowed at the screaming crowd before promptly stepping on mini Buckingham Palace, turning it to rubble, '**AAAARRRGH!**' came my frustrated cry.

RUN FOR YOUR LIVES!

Gosh, this Poowong Big Head must actually be real. Why else would everybody be stampeding away?

'**WAIT FOR MEEEEEE!**' I yelled trying to keep up with the fleeing crowd. '**UUUUUNNNNGGGGHHHH! MY HEAD HURTS!**'

The screaming had escalated from plain old terror to hysterical panic. Which made me panic and topple into the the mini windmill. People were going berko every which way I turned.

It's going to **DESTROY** US ALL!

RUUUUUN!

OK, now I didn't care if Dad was about to birdie, I had to find my parents because quite frankly, this was gettting frighteningly frightening.

'**MUUUUUUM! DAAAAAD! I CAAAAAN'T SEEEEE!**' I called out in the hope they might be nearby.

'**OH GOD, IT'S GOT PARENTS!**' someone yelled.

'THERE'S A *FAMILY* OF THEM!' yelled someone else.

SOMEBODY CALL THE **ZOO!**

WHAT? A family of them? What was I up against? I ran and **SMASH! CRASH!** Hope nobody was too attached to the mini Sydney Harbour Bridge. **CRACK! BANG!** The mini Sphinx was crushed. I hope there's no mini curses that went with that. **OOF!** Something hit me straight in the stomach and I tumbled over whatever it was, bringing it down with me. I looked up, barely able to make out my parents looking down upon me.

'ARRGH! IT'S ZEE **POOVONG BIG HEDT!** IT HASS BRUNG DOWN ZEE **BERLIN VALL** IN VUN SMALL STEP! RUN BEFORE IT *KILLS US ALL!*

THE POOWONG BIG HEAD LIVES!

The next thing I remember is Mum cradling me in her lap, 'Tracy, can you hear me? Tracy?'

'Mum, the Poowong Big Head is on the loose and . . .'

'You're the POOWONG BIG HEAD, darling.'

Huh? Brain thinking, thinking . . . Ohhhhhhh, me with the head of epic proportions, crawling out of the swamp covered in all that goop and the mass of destruction that followed . . .

FLASH! FLASH! FLASH! Suddenly the media were all over us, snapping photos, firing questions.

FLASH! FLASH! FLASH! FLASH!

How does it feel to have tamed the famous POOWONG BIG HEAD?

Does it speak ENGLISH?

Who's its favourite DESIGNER?

'She's not some animal, she's a human being!' my mum yelled in her **ANGRY MUM VOICE**, scaring them away. 'Are you OK, darling?'

I told her my head hurt.

'Could you hang on for four more holes?'

Just **FOUR** more holes?

'Zen vee vill call ze ambulance, vee promise.' I hoped an apology was to follow these ridiculous statements, which I may or may not have hallucinated, but I blacked out so I guess I'll never know.

AND IN OTHER NEWS . . .

That night, with the lounge decorated ready for Mum and Dad's **IMPENDING VICTORY**, we sat among the balloons and streamers like a bunch of sad sacks.

My giant head was too heavy to sit on my shoulders without the help of a neck brace. Worse still, until the swelling went down, I was stuck in the 'Team Lacy, Here To Kick Up A Storm' T-shirt. Pff, Kick Up a Storm? We sure did. It was all over the news.

'There I am!' Leif yelled. 'Right behind the Poowong Big Head!' And indeed he was, pulling **rabbit ears** because obviously I didn't look ridiculous enough.

As they wheeled me onto the ambulance, with the double doors open so they could squeeze my **massive cranium** through, a reporter stood at my side doing his piece to the camera in his stupid reporter voice.

'A young girl who crawled out of the mini swamp of New Orleans or the real Poowong Big Head? You be the judge!'

A giant close-up of my head **filled the screen**. Or was it just that my head was **so giant** it filled the screen? Suddenly none of that mattered, for there on the telly for the world to see, **BOMO** was at my side … and then they cut.

WHAT?!! But ... but ... no-one got to see the good bit, the bit I will remember **forever**. The bit where, in a moment of **MARVELLOUS MARVELLOUSNESS**, I briefly regained consciousness and looked up **marvelling** at **BOMO**. 'Hopefully we'll see each other again,' I said.

'**Maybe**,' he said as the doors of the ambulance closed.

'Maybe' was our word. '**He said our word. He said maybe. He likes me!**' I said to the paramedic.

HE LIKES ME

'Patient **incoherent** and **hallucinating**. Sirens on, move it on out!'

I drifted off to the **WOO-WOO-WOO** of the siren and the **THUMP THUMP THUMP** of my head.

But back to the TV where another news story was running . . . the one about the couple who were set to be the first to win three minigolf tournaments blah, blah, etc, etc, **WE KNOW ALREADY!** The owner of 'Around the World in 18 Holes' spoke to the reporter, 'We were set to make Poowong history today and look at this place! Ruined! That Poowong Big Head klutz . . . I'm sorry . . . I can't go on!'

I'm sorry . . . I can't go on!

It was bad enough that a grown man was **crying on television** but even worse, it was all because of me. Well, it wasn't half-obvious with everyone in the room staring at me. I tried to do the big doe-eyed 'I'm innocent' look, but given my eyes couldn't open more than two millimetres, I looked more like an unrepentant **hardened criminal.**

'Oh, come on,' I pleaded. 'They've agreed to a rematch once the place is fixed . . . next summer.'

A **deathly silence** which I silently begged for someone to fill. Yes, it hurt to open my mouth, but I was willing to suffer the pain of making small talk because I knew this silence was actually saying something, and that something was **'THIS IS ALL YOUR FAULT, TRACY LACY!'**

'You know vhat?' Dad said, cutting through the vibe of the blame. 'Our Tracy is right. She ist here und alife und that is vhat matters, yah?'

'You're right, darling,' my mum said as she kissed my forehead, **'Jeez, your head is huge, isn't it?'**

And then we partied, as if Mum and Dad were the **minigolf champions** they so hoped to be.

I mean, no use moping among all these decorations and letting that food go to waste. Everyone waited on me hand and foot, which I rather enjoyed.

And the whole incident was put to rest.

At least I thought so until ...

THE NEXT MORNING . . .

OK, now we could put everything to rest. At least I thought so until ...

LATER . . .

THANK GOODNESS we were leaving. Now I
could really put everything to rest. At least I thought
so until . . .

A BIT LATER THAN LATER . . .

It was the **rainbow-farting pink pony** incident of Grade One, only bigger and it was never going to go away.

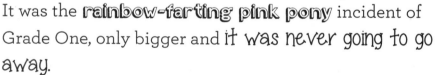

SIDE-THOUGHT: Find brilliant excuse to not holiday in Poowong for next 10 years. Maybe even 20. **END SIDE-THOUGHT**

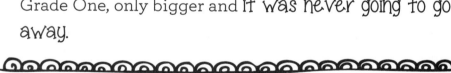

Hey Boofhead, did some research. Turns out sometimes the swelling never, ever goes down. Don't worry, you could always offer yourself to science research.

That's funny, Leif, I researched stories on sisters who sought revenge on their brothers for reading their diaries and your day is coming.

Day **36** of **SUMMER** holidays

7 days to start of **HIGH SCHOOL**

1 day back from **POOWONG**. May I **NEVER** return or have my knickers set on **FIRE!**

HOME IS WHERE THE HEART IS

BLEURGH! Within 24 hours of walking into the house it was like we'd **never been** on holiday. As far as Mum was concerned it was **all systems go!**

My Poowong adventures with Ag and Ponky, along with our **successes** and **failures** and **more failures**, and might as well throw in **a couple more of those failures**, seemed so far away now. **HEAVY SIGH!**

SIDE-THOUGHT: I can't help but feel those failures were in some way significantly significant. I don't know how or why, it just feels like that. **END SIDE-THOUGHT**

SIDE-SIDE-THOUGHT: Maybe that's why Ag and Ponky and me **feel so weird**. We **failed so much** but we **didn't feel** like **failures** at all. **END SIDE-SIDE-THOUGHT**

SIDE-SIDE-SIDE-THOUGHT: All our mums are being really annoying. I guess it could have something to do with the fact we start high school in ... **7 MORE DAYS!!!!!** **END SIDE-SIDE-SIDE-THOUGHT**

FLASH FLASH FLASH

FLASH! FLASH! Yes, the words are **FLASHING! FLASH! FLASH! BRIGHT GREEN NEON-TYPE FLASHING! FLASH! FLASH!** With pink neon Oomphoofs leaping around it with **FLASHING RAINBOWS** coming out of their butts. Kinda like this . . .

7 MORE DAYS

OK, it's not flashing but if it did, it would be the **AMAZINGEST** neon sign in the history of the world.

207

ANNOYING MUMS UNITE!

I guess with **7 DAYS UNTIL THE START OF HIGH SCHOOL** we should have expected our mums to transform into **mumzillas**. **WHY?** Because of ...

THE SCHOOL-READY EXPEDITION

Yes, that **strange phenomenon** which takes place in every shopping mall the world over. I knew the day was coming. The **dreaded 'SCHOOL-READY' shopping EXPEDITION**. It's easy to recognise—**CRAZY mums**, crazily waving a long list in the air, shouting as they drag us kids behind them.

'Hurry up, I want to get to the **shoe shop** before the queue's out the door.'

This **day-long expedition** for books, pens, pencils, notebooks, uniforms and shoes (of course) can **break the strongest of children**.

SIDE-THOUGHT: What is it with mothers and 'quality' school shoes?

'WE NEED TO GET GOOD-QUALITY SUPPORTIVE SHOES.'

'We need room to grow, but they have to be quality.'

'I don't care if they don't look cool, I'm paying for quality.'

END SIDE-THOUGHT

We were all wearily well-versed in this annual shopping black hole but nothing could have prepared Ponky, Ag and I for the pain that comes with . . .

THE HIGH-SCHOOL-READY SHOPPING EXPEDITION!

The High-School-Ready Shopping Expedition was
so bad that me, Ag and Ponky realised our previous
experience was NOTHING! NOTHING! NOTHING!
compared to this because . . .

1. 'High-School-Ready Shopping' was probably a
    hundred times worse than going to high school.
    (YES, IT IS <u>THAT</u> BAD!)

2. High-School-Ready Shopping required its own
    program, like OBULOG only more hardcore.

3. Good old number three. I have nothing for
    number three.

Afterwards a DEUM-NEGI debrief was required . . .
in where else but THE LOUNGE (DA-DA DA-DAAA!)
where we knew we could speak freely, and speak
freely we did!

It was HORRIBLE!

I wanted to RUN!

I wanted to die!...

She held giant whitie derpants against my clothes to see if they fit...

Socks, you could have sworn we were choosing diamonds...

Giant whitie UNDERPANTS, infront of everyone!...

She's actually making my uniform!...

And these boys were HUGE!

Don't get me started on the shoe shop!...

I hid in the dressing room!...

kept making excuses go to the toilet!...

She held the trousers infront of my crotch, measuring...

We'd taken a number but they hadn't served us....

But she's actually making my uniform!

air, they had back hair! I just lost it....

She's actually making my uniform!

Measuring my crotch! Infront of everyone!

Woah! EVERYONE, BREATHE!

'By the sounds of things,' I said, 'We all need to take turns to share the pain our mothers put us through today.'

ME FIRST

'It's bad enough I have to go to a school where the school colours are PURPLE AND GOLD, but I did not for one second think my mother WOULD BE MAKING said purple-striped dress!'

She's actuall MAKING m UNIFORM!

'What's the big deal?' Ag and Ponky asked.

'What's the big deal? Really? FIRST OF ALL, when Mum made Leif's high school uniform, she decided to use some old patterns she had in her sewing room. Long story short, Leif attended his first day of high school in flared pants and a 70s-style shirt. He might as well have walked into the school with 'Please feel free to make my life a living hell' tattooed across his forehead.

SECOND OF ALL, Mum insisted on buying the best-quality material which looks completely different from the material of the 'Made in China' uniforms.

And THIRD OF ALL, she had to pick the pattern of the style that NOBODY at the school wears.

So THE BIG DEAL is it takes one quarter of a second for people to form an opinion of you, a quarter of a second I cannot afford to be wasted on my HOMEMADE UNIFORM.'

Suddenly Ag and Ponky got it. They shook their heads in disbelief.

Ag said the shoe shop was packed as in 'take a number, we'll serve you in order' packed. But when their number was finally called, no-one saw her mum waving the ticket or heard her saying, 'Yes, 47 over here.' (Ah-huh, knew it! NINJA GENES!) Anyway, Ag said the shop assistant went straight to 48 and Ag said she's so used to thinking OBULOG in every situation, she just had to do something. She walked straight up to 48 and said 'Excuse me 48, maybe you didn't see us, we're 47.' But 48 steam-rolled right over Ag, demanding some good-quality school shoes for her daughter. (Again with the quality footwear!) 'I just couldn't let it go,' Ag said. 'I'm sorry 48,' she continued, 'but as far

as I'm aware 47 COMES BEFORE 48 and has done so for centuries.' And then 48 turned to Ag and her mum and said, 'You missed your chance 47.' Then Ag said she was dragged out by security.

'WHAT?' we said.

'WHAT?' we said again.

'Well,' Ag said, 'I remembered when I was in primary school and the very first time I counted to 100 without skipping a number I got a gold star. A gold star! And you know why? Because every number deserved to be counted. You don't just skip over a number so you can get to 100 quicker, you have to give each number its moment. I wanted my moment!'

'GET TO THE BIT ABOUT BEING DRAGGED OUT BY THE SECURITY GUARD!!!'

'Oh that,' Ag said. 'I said to 48, how about I serve you so we can get you back to the **alternate number counting reality** from **whence you came** . . . and then I threw a shoe at her.'

I threw a shoe at her!

'Beg pardon?'

'I threw a shoe at her!'

'IN THE NAME OF QUALITY FOOTWEAR, WHAT?' I said.

'It wasn't at her **head or anything**, it was at her feet but yes, I threw it.'

We were just getting our heads around this concept when Ag sent us spiralling further into shock.

'And I **enjoyed it**, the **POWER**, even if it did only last for a second, because that's when the security guard arrived and dragged me out. But if he hadn't, I might have thrown more shoes because I think ... OBULOG HAS TURNED ME INTO A MONSTER!'

I AM A MONSTER!

'No it hasn't,' said a quiet voice from the corner. Ponky and I jumped out of our chairs. It was Ag's mum! She'd been there the whole time!!! BEJINGY-JINGOES, what is wrong with that family? 'I just want to see if Ag's good-quality school shoes fit. I had to guess the size after she was, er-hem ... removed.'

Ag immediately apologised to her mum for her behaviour and then her mum said the most beautiful thing ever. 'Darling, I was so proud of you standing up for us. I would advise against throwing things, but with a little more practise, you'll find the control you need to be able to STAND UP AND BE COUNTED.'

Ponky and I turned to Ag, 'Your mum is so **cool**!' But when we turned back . . . her mum was gone. This woman wasn't just a ninja, she was the NINJA MASTER.

Your **MUM** is SO COOL!

'Do the shoes fit, Ag?' she called from outside the window. What-the-be-jingo! How did she get there so fast? Anyway, we all agreed that yes, Ag had gone too far but like the ninja master said, with a bit of practise, she'll be able to HAVE HER MOMENT without the need for projectile footwear.

And PONKY told us his story of woe . . .

'So we walked into the uniform shop and this friend of Mum's was there. Her son is starting at Northwood High—SAME YEAR AS US. I was about to walk into the dressing room when this giant guy walks out complaining the shirt is too small. It was the son, Mum's friend's son. He stripped off his shirt, and . . .'

Ponky suddenly stopped, gathered himself and blurted it out, 'He had back hair!'

'So?' Ag and I asked.

'SO? SO? Everywhere I looked, there were weird hairy man-boys and they're all going into the first year of high school with me ... WITH BACK HAIR ...' Oh, now we were getting the picture. 'I don't have hair like that, I'm half their height and my name is Ponky. They all had names like Matt, Dom, Pete, manly names. Does Ponky sound MANLY to you?'

BACK HAIR!

'Well ... um ... Ag, what do you ...?'

'It doesn't matter! The days of Ponky are gone! From this moment I will only answer to my real name!'

Ag mouthed at me 'what is his real name?'.

'IT'S MARCUS!!!' Ponky screamed.

Oh boy, this was a big problem. It wasn't just me and Ag who would have to rewire our brains to call him Marcus, it was everyone we knew that was going to Northwood High. This was INSANE, RILUDICROUS, ABSURDULOUS! UNLESS...

'I've got it! The answer to all our problems!'

Is this an invite I see before me? Thank you, yes. I would love to come.

Please do . . . NOT EVEN CONSIDER FOR ONE MOMENT COMING TO THIS PARTY!!!

Bathers? Check.

♡ 2 days to start of HIGH SCHOOL ♡

ULTERIOR MOTIVE? WHO US?

This was the best idea ever and we knew it. And, I admit there were some TEENSY HICCUPS at the party but . . . well, before I get to that, we had the party at Ponk . . . Marcus's house because if there's one thing I know, if you send out an invite with the word 'pool' on it, kids will march like pilgrims to this great body of water.

The day before, P . . . Marcus, Ag and I went through **OUR GOALS**. Oh yes, there was a **very definite reason** for having this party and it had **nothing to do** with fun.

We invited everyone we knew from primary school who was going to Northwood High. Thus, therefore and . . . (oops, nearly!) the dress code was strictly Northwood High uniform. Sure, it sounded fun on the invite, all of us **rocking up in our uniforms**, feeling all **high schoolie**, but there was an **ULTERIOR MOTIVE**. For me this party was a way to **reveal** my **homemade, best-quality fabric, style that nobody ever wears** uniform in the hope that

1. It would prevent shock, finger-pointing or discussion on the first day.

2. I would have a chance to talk it up, maybe even to a point where others might want to wear it.

3. Why are you always so hard, number three?

Then there was the other ulterior motive—giving Ag a social situation where she might find an opportunity to practise the control her ninja master suggested ... which basically means not throwing the nearest object while basking in the power of power. We can't have Ag believing any progress she has made with OBULOG has turned her into A MONSTER.

And finally, the other, other ulterior motive … and perhaps the hardest … the introduction of the person who, from this day forward, would be known as MARCUS. Personally, short of hiring a hypnotist, I felt we stood very little chance of having the name 'Ponky' obliterated from everyone's memory but Ponk… Marcus was convinced he could do it. I guess the thought of the hairy man-boys laughing at him was all the motivation he needed.

And finally, finally the other, other, other ulterior motive was, as always, to keep OBULOG at the forefront of our minds at all times. This party would reveal just how far we had come and we were positively peeing our pants over it.

PARTY PREP

After spending the morning blowing up balloons and hanging streamers in Ponk... (this is never going to work) Marcus's backyard, we stood back, looked at our **creative genius** and thought, yep, **decorating is definitely not** one of our strong points. Yes it was colourful, a lot like a clown had run around the yard **spewing up** kind of colourful. But with just 30 minutes to 'party time', **COLOURED CLOWN-SPEW** it would remain. It was time to dress for the big event.

MY GRAND ENTRANCE ...

UNIFORM ON, one last glance in the mirror and I have to say, **it didn't look that bad.**

As I walked back to Pon . . . arcus's house I heard the OONCE-OONCE-OONCE! of the music and the excited babble of an already PUMPING PARTY. I'd given my entrance some thought—the big TA-DAA! or a simple walk and mingle. I'd decided to go with the simple walk and mingle, hopeful I could casually slip the topic of my uniform into conversation as I served the party pies. 'Yes, it is LOVELY FABRIC. It's the best-quality fabric money can buy.' 'That's the problem with uniforms, they all look the same, but this one . . .' 'This uniform gives me a sense of individualness.' 'The Made in China uniforms didn't come close.' Yes, my simple walk and mingle approach would also fit in nicely with OBULOG . . . to be exact, point 2. Show-off-free zone.

And so upon arrival, I indiscreetly made my indiscreet entrance to the pool area. Oh, and that thing I said about my uniform not looking bad . . . I take it back. The purple stripes were way more purple than anyone else's.

I was a **PURPLE-STRIPED BEACON.** And . . . my mum insisted the dress be hemmed at mid-calf because that's what the pattern recommended. EVERYONE ELSE HAD THEIRS ABOVE THE KNEE! I looked like I'd stepped out of a **time machine** from somewhere a **VERY, VERY** long time ago—maybe as far back as the 1950s.

PURPLE STRIPE BEACON

I had to get to Ag and Pon . . . cus who were of course at the other end of the pool. I **ducked** from giant fern to potted palm, hiding in the hibiscus bush hissing for Ag and Po . . . rcus.

'GUYS! HELP!'

They took one look at me.

'Sticky tape, STAT!' Ag ordered. Ponky raced inside, Ag dragging me from the hibiscus bush insisting, *'No-one will notice, now come on!'* I stepped out from the bush. The babble of the pumping party suddenly de-babbled with **EVERYONE** literally staring at me, their eyes running down the length of my uniform, which took a really long time considering how long it was.

WHY DID MUM HAVE TO MAKE MY UNIFORM? WHY? WHY?

'Hi everyone,' I stalled, trying to somehow make this better.

'AHHHHHHHHH!' I exhaled, stretching my arms up as high as I could, raising my hemline a good two centimetres. 'Tired? You bet. Just going to take a quick nap.' I **scurried** through the crowd into the house, arms above my head the entire way in what must have been the world's longest yawn.

YAWWWWNNNNN!

Ag securely taped up my uniform to an acceptable length. Now it was time to get to work selling the idea of its **superior form** and **quality**, a job now made more difficult given my entrance in the evening gown version of the uniform. But of course, it would be too much to ask that ANYTHING would go my way. I returned to the party to find a circle of people in **fits of laughter** and who should be in the centre of said circle? GEOF? I knew he'd be telling a story about me, making me look even more completely coo-coo

bananas just when I'd spent my entire holiday trying to **COMPLETELY UN-COO-COO BANANA** myself. Plus he had **so much dirt** on me from reading my diary!

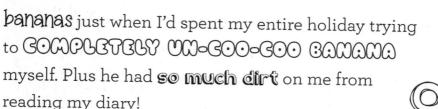

ENOUGH! ENOUGH! ENOUGH!

'Leif, so sorry to interrupt,' I said, 'Mum says you have to go home. She has to put the ointment on your boils, the ones **on your bottom**. She doesn't want you to get in the pool and infect everyone else.'

Laughter **gone**, everyone **BACKING AWAY** like he had **the plague**.

'I told you I would make you pay for reading my diary,' I whispered in his ear, then suddenly noticed the look on his face, which looked an awful lot like hurt.

'Jeez, Tracy, I was just telling them about my first day at high school in my 70s uniform.'

UGH, way to make a sister feel bad. And it was during this bad feeling that a million images of Leif's life suddenly flashed through my mind. There was something particularly particular about them and that particular-ness was my brother Leif is always alone. There are NO FRIENDS or people he hangs with, he's never brought anyone over. Even on holiday, he would sooner go fishing than be at the ice-cream parlour with all the other kids.

MY BROTHER LEIF IS A LONER!

How had I not realised this? No wonder he's always mucking about with me. And no wonder he's never tread the path or pushed the boundaries, he's had no reason to because Leif's path is one **HE WALKS ALONE**. And the weird bit, **he's OK with it**.

'**WAIT, COME BACK! I'M ONLY KIDDING!**' I yelled to his posse of listeners. 'The story Leif should be telling you is the one about the Poowong Big Head.'

Suddenly they were back, eyes wide with excitement, waiting for Leif to continue. Oh boy, I was about to become a laughing stock all over again.

WHAT HAD I DONE?

'Oh yes, you mean ...'

I held my breath, waiting for him to say my name ...

'... **COUSIN TINA!**'

Cousin **TINA!**

'YES! **COUSIN TINA!** Of course that's who I meant! What a giant ning-nong she is. Seems to run in the family.'

I looked at Leif, relieved. Leif looked at me, grateful ... before quietly adding, 'Don't think for one second you're completely off the hook.'

'I wouldn't have it any other way,' I smiled as I left Leif to have his moment in the sun.

SIDE-THOUGHT: How could we be so different? No wonder Mum says we're like chalk and cheese. Will be taking a closer look at this loner chalk situation. END SIDE-THOUGHT

SIDE-SIDE-THOUGHT: I am assuming I am the cheese. END SIDE-SIDE-THOUGHT

BUT WHY WAS EVERYONE HERE?

Ag and I were wandering through the crowd, proud that we'd brought all our FRIENDS TOGETHER, when suddenly I thought ... given our less than impressive score on the HA-YA SCALE, what was everyone doing here?

'I don't know,' Ag said out of the blue. (She's reading my mind now???)

I thought for sure someone would have poked fun at me over my uniform bizzo. But no, not so much as a sneaky whisper ... FROM ANYONE!! My entrance was already forgotten!??! And given no-one had said anything about the incidents of my primary school years, I think it was safe to assume all that was forgotten too.

'I know, it's SO weird,' Ag added. (OK, the sudden ninja mind-reading ability was FREAKING ME OUT. Ag's powers are developing rapidly. I have no idea where it's leading but it will require close monitoring.)

Here I was, having just spent the ENTIRE HOLIDAYS trying to unlearn talking, thinking and obsessing about myself and now it's the 'in thing.'

'That's it! Can you smell it?' I asked Ag.

'Smell what?'

'Hormones! The air is thick with hormones. It's arrived,' I said.

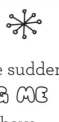

'What's arrived?'

'Puberty, Ag, PUBERTY!' I declared with 100% certain certainty.

Everyone was so obsessed with themselves, I'm pretty sure the two of us could have walked through that party with carnations growing out of our heads. Yes, everyone would laugh but only until the worry kicked in: 'If I laugh, do my teeth look okay?', 'Will my hair remain in place if I throw my head back and laugh?', 'If I point and laugh, will anyone notice my nails aren't painted?' According to the one-and-a-half self-help books I had read, this was perfectly normal adolescent behaviour.

'My eyebrows did actually meet in the middle,' said Sally to Annette as Ag and I happened by.

'Is she a werewolf?' Ag whispered to me.

'So Mum waxed it and turned my giant hairy monobrow into two eyebrows.'

My eyebrows did actually meet in the middle

Is she a werewolf?

What? Puberty can make your *eyebrows grow together?* Ag and I checked each other's. PHEW! Still had two.

Training BRA

'It's called a **training bra**,' Natalie said discreetly to her friend. 'Mum said I need to wear one now, what with the sudden growth spurt.'

'What does that even mean?' I said.

'Maybe it **comes with wheels?**' Ag said, just as CONFUSED as me.

'I have **one hair**, on my chest. Does that make me pre-pubescent?' Davin asked his mates.

EWWWWWWW!!

OK, obviously a large part of puberty is about HAIR. Did we need to buy a hedge trimmer, Ag and I wondered.

'I don't know that I like the sound of puberty,' Ag confided.

'Well, there's just some things we can't control,' I said with a strange sense of the heebie-jeebies.

AND INTRODUCING . . .

'Thanks so much for coming, this is so much fun,' Ponk . . . Marcus said to everyone. He sounded slightly like a nervous politician but strangely convincing at the same time. Ag and me were so proud. This was a brave move that could go one of two ways . . .

Everyone was listening so intently. My urge to put on a mini-musical was suddenly so strong I found it hard to concentrate. **Cheesey-cheeses** they were a captive audience, who wouldn't want to seize the moment?

I'm TRACY of the
LACY see how I
kick my legs
REALLY HIGH ...
I LOVE to
DANCE and
SING and ...
hey wait! Get
back here!!!

Sadly, I knew the days of entertaining my fellow students with my **dazzling performances** were gone ... unless of course I did an **interpretive dance piece** of a sprouting hair. EWWWWWWW!

'I know we're all moving on to this new experience called high school,' Pon ... cus said interrupting my daydream, 'but I want to TRULY move on and to do that I need your help. Ummm ... I want ... well, I was wondering ... it's just that ...' Uh-oh, this was heading in the un-hero direction. 'I ... ah ... I ...' I could see Ponky desperately needed my help, but could I get up there and help him without busting some moves and bursting into song?

'What Ponky is TRYING to say is we all grow up,' I said immediately grabbing their attention but desperately wanting to throw a few spectacularly spectacular moves in to really, really grab their attention. 'I mean, everyone has been talking about it here today. Sally, with her monobrow, Natalie with her new training bra and Davin with his one hair.'

Oh dear, they were glaring at me ...

'OBVIOUSLY information you wanted to remain private, so moving on ... part of Ponky growing up is that he would like you to call him by his real name, which is ... Mmmm ... Mmmm ... (deep breath, I can do this) MARCUS! So much better than Ponky, I'm sure you'll agree. I mean, who in the name of names, who would want to go to high school with a name that sounds like it belongs to A REALLY CUTE SOFT TOY? So let's get that name into our heads and give Marcus here a fighting chance.

MARCUS! MARCUS! MARCUS!

Soon the entire party was chanting... **'MAR-CUS! MAR-CUS! MAR-CUS!'** I looked at Marcus who smiled at me. He somehow **seemed taller.** And then my need to perform for the crowd overtook me and I started dancing to the happy chant of his name,

MAR-CUS'!

MAR-CUS! MAR-CUS! MAR-CUS!

I was just getting into it when...

'**STOP!**' came a cry from the back of the crowd.

STOP!

It was Effie, a small and timid girl. In fact, she was so small and timid that until this moment I'd never heard her say anything other than 'here' at morning roll-call. As you can imagine, her big voice came as a shock to everyone.

'You've been so brave, Marcus, and **inspired me** to ask that I too be called by my real name.'

'**YAY! WOO-HOO!**' everyone cheered at Effie's new found gutsiness.

'Please call me ...'
we waited as she drew
breath to say it ...
'**FROGMEENA! MY NAME
IS FROGMEENA!**'

'**FROGMEENA!**'

'**YAAAAAAAY!**' the crowd cheered.
'**FROG-MEE-NA! FROG-HUH?** ...'

Awkward!

Crickets chirp.

CHIRP

Tumbleweeds blow through.

This was the awkwardest 'awkward silence' I had ever heard (or un-heard?). Everyone knew Effie had made a really bad choice, but no-one was saying it. Silence... **more silence** ... going on for a **REALLY LONG TIME** and we all know how I hate silence of the long, awkward kind. It had to be done, it had to be fixed... **OBULOG** Tracy, think of **OBULOG**. But no, I had to do something...

'But Effie is such a **great name!**' I yelled enthusiastically. '**EFF-IE! EFF-IE! EFF-IE!** Just join in when the vibe takes you,' I shouted at the still-stunned crowd.

EFF-IE!

EFF-IE!

EFF-IE!

Slowly but surely, '**EFFIE! EFFIE! EFFIE!**', the chant growing louder and louder with what I'm sure was a sense of relief that I'd saved Effie from a **lifetime of mockery.** 'No need to thank me,' I said as I hugged her.

'*Something something* the name Effie!' is all I heard as I walked on. Not sure what the '*something something*' was. It sounded a lot like 'I hate', but I doubt it.

My work here was done, **Marcus** was **Marcus** and bonus, **Effie** was **not Frogmeena**, so now it was time for party pies and sausage rolls.

WHOOP! WHOOP! WHOOP! **LET'S GO!**

I FROZE.

There is only one person who says that!

'I, FOR EXAMPLE, WILL BE GOING TO A PRIVATE SCHOOL' rang in my ears as clear as the day Victoria Fuller had said it, yet here she was **IN A NORTHWOOD HIGH UNIFORM!** At **OUR** party! **HOW DARE SHE!**

Ag and (I hate saying it, I hate saying it, it's the last time I'm going to say 'I hate saying it . . .') Marcus were already at my side begging the question, 'Why is **she** here?' There were only three possible answers:

Why is <u>she</u> here?

1. She was a spy.

2. She was making fun of us.

3. Why can I never come up with a third reason for anything?

Anyway, it **didn't matter why** she was here. What mattered was **she was here.** 'It doesn't matter why she's here...' I said, realising it would be better to **share my thoughts out loud.** 'She's not going to Northwood High so that makes her a **GATECRASHER.'**

Brain ticking over, **TICK! TICK! TOCK!**

'Ag, time for you to do as your **ninja master** instructed.'

'My who?'

'Never mind, you have an opportunity here **to stand up for yourself,** for **the real** Northwood High students, to **practise self-control** while **asserting yourself**, like your mum said. Now go, my little ninja!'

> Now **GO,** my little NINJA!

Ag looked me as though I was nuts. I turned to Marcus (see, not mentioning anything about his **crappy new name**) giving him the **you explain** glance. We turned back but Ag was **GONE**, already at Victoria's side. How in the **name of time-bending** did she . . . no time to think about that right now, **because Victoria Fuller was sobbing**.

WHAT HAD AG DONE?

SOB!

'I just asked her to leave,' Ag explained, 'and she started crying. I **didn't throw** anything!' Oh boy, this was going to be a true test of **OBULOG** for all of us. We had to **comfort** Victoria, but she was just as likely to **punch us** in the face for our efforts.

'My parents lost **all their money** on the stock exchange. We're so **impoverished** they **can't afford** to send me to a private schoo-oo-ool.' Victoria wept. 'Now I have to go to Northwood with the rest of you people.'

YOU PEOPLE? **YOU PEOPLE?**

Let it go, Tracy, let it go . . .

Noticing my eyes narrowing, Marcus stepped in. 'Victoria, that's **terrible**. Is there **ANYTHING** we can do to help? Take up a collection, donate food, clothing?'

'Ohhhh, **that's so cute,** but Dad said once we've sold **TWO** of our **three holiday homes**, that should tide us over.'

WHAT??????????????

Holey cheeses, save us. Was she really saying this?

She started blubbering again. 'The worst bit is we have to sell the one in Fra-a-a-ance! I can see you're all just as upset as me.'

Er, no we weren't! There was no hint of 'upset' from us. But Victoria seemed to think our stares of 'there are no words to describe how loony this is' were stares of understanding. And her blubbery blubbering continued!

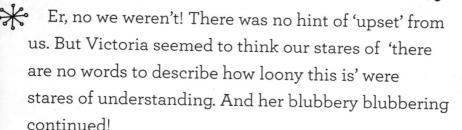

'It's so nice to have friends who understand how **DISTRESSING** it is that you may never ski in Aspen ag-ai-ai-ain.'

Er, no we didn't and the looks on our faces fell somewhere between 'are you for real' and 'please get out of our faces right now!' Somehow Victoria interpreted this as an invite to stay.

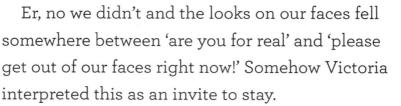

'Not living the life to which I've become accustomed is going to be so hard. I guess the only good thing is that now that I'm poor, I qualify as a guest at your party.'

OW! OW! From the corner of my eye, I caught a glimpse of Ag **angrily slamming** a balloon into her hand. 'Step away from the balloon, Ag, no good can come of this.'

Before any of us knew what was happening, Ag was bopping Victoria over the head with the balloon, an **angry bop** for every **angry syllable** . . .

Look up the meaning of **POV-ER-TY** in the **DIC-TION-AR-Y!!!**

'How **DARE** you . . .' Victoria began, but before she could compose herself to continue, Ag was already boxing her around the ears . . . with words thankfully.

'No, how dare you, Victoria! You think you have nothing?! See this balloon, right now it's something!' Ag popped it. 'Now it's nothing. This is what NOTHING LOOKS LIKE.' Ag stormed away.

Victoria looked like she was about to burst into tears again, but not 'I'm so poor tears', more like 'I'm so embarrassed someone just bopped me on the head with a balloon' tears.

All in all, I would say it was a fairly successful outcome. Ag was controlled in her use of the balloon, while clearly asserting herself. And Victoria was suitably embarrassed . . . for maybe a split second.

'Well, those party pies and sausage rolls aren't going to serve themselves,' I said grabbing Ponk . . . ugh . . . Marcus by the arm and racing towards the kitchen.

'Ag was so cool!' Marcus whispered gleefully.

'Cooler than an iceberg!' We were proud she was our best friend.

HE WALKED INTO THE PARTY . . .

THWAAACH-IISSSHHH!

That was the sound I made as I took a **full belly-whack** into the pool. A plume of water shot up into the air and plop-plop-plop-plop-plop-plop the party pies and sausage rolls rained down upon me before **DONK!** the tray landed on my head.

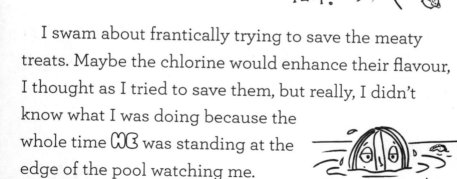

I swam about frantically trying to save the meaty treats. Maybe the chlorine would enhance their flavour, I thought as I tried to save them, but really, I didn't know what I was doing because the whole time OB was standing at the edge of the pool watching me.

'**TRACY?**' he said.

Now, I'm not sure if anyone else has ever experienced this. It was definitely a first for me. I knew something **really awful** was happening but suddenly it was as though I was looking down on myself, seeing every moment in **microscopic detail**, wishing there was a way to stop it, change it, rewind it.

Everything started going wrong when I turned to offer party pies and sausage rolls to some kids and turned straight into . . .

And that's when everything went into . . .

SLOOOOOOW MOOOOTION

SLOOOOOOW MOOOOTION REEEEEPLAY

Reel back in horror at sight of BOMO, left foot tries to stop horror-reel but realise tray is frisbee-ing towards him. Manage to grab tray but overcorrect to regain balance. Right foot moves behind left to correct overcorrection but strong sense I'm falling backwards hits me. I spin 180 DEGREES to regain balance, stepping forward to steady self on solid ground only there is NO GROUND, just water. Brain registers 'I'm falling into pool'.

NOOOOOOOOOOOOOOO–'

Throw tray into the air in hope of saving food. Continue fall . . .

'–OOOOOOOOOOOO
OOOOOOOOOOOOOOO
OOOOOOOOOOOOOOO
OOOOOOOOOOOOOOO
OOOOOOOOOOOOOOO

OOOOOOOOOOOOOOOOOOOOOOOOOOOOO
OOOOOOOOOOOO–' halfway to point of impact
'–OOOOOOOOOOOOOOOOOOOOOOOO
OOOOOOOOOOOOOOOOOOOOOOOO
OO–' grabbing at air whilst fully aware this will **end**

badly '–OOOOOOOOOOOOOO
OOOOOOOOOOOOOOOOOOOOOO
OOOOOOOOOOOOOOOOOOOOOO
OOOOOOOOOOOOOOOOOOOOOO

OOOOOOOOOOOOOOOOOO–' Tip of
nose touches water. Time freezes.

★ SIDE-THOUGHT: Why was BOMO here? END SIDE- ★
★ THOUGHT ★

THWAAACH-IISSSHHH!

> **SIDE-SIDE-THOUGHT**: Why was he in a Northwood High uniform? **END SIDE-SIDE-THOUGHT**

SIDE-SIDE-SIDE-THOUGHT: I would need air at some point but was *too embarrassed* to surface. **END SIDE-SIDE-THOUGHT**

Seems a person's natural instinct to breathe overrides any fear of embarrassment. I hit the surface and began my rescue of the bite-sized morsels in the pool. Out of the corner of my eye, I could see ⒷⓄⓂⓄ with Cunners, leaning over the edge of the pool.

'You *KNOW* her? She's the one I was telling you about,' Cunners laughed.

He could laugh all he wanted because I knew BOMO was about to put him right back in his box.

'No . . . I mean, we met once,' BOMO said following Cunners like a little puppy. He didn't even glance back to see if I was OK.

I pulled myself out of the pool. The tape from my uniform hem was tangled tightly around my legs so I could only take the tiniest of steps. I'd like to think I looked like a gorgeous mermaid teetering across the pool tiles but no, I was a drowned rat caught in a mess of sticky tape and a frock from times gone by.

If the same thing happened to someone else, they would probably want to curl up in a corner and cry. I am not one of those people. I did however think this would be the perfect opportunity to reorganise Ponky's mum's pantry using the dewey decimal system—that's the system they use to categorise books at the library. Ag and Ponky found me there, surrounded by food items. They tried very hard to comfort me but I told them I was fine and Marcus should tell his mum all flours and grains would be on the shelf marked 'FLO.000 through to GRA.001'.

Ag said that BOMO had just moved here from Queensland and was going to be a student at Northwood.

'Fantastic,' I said, ignoring the steady drip of pool water

FANTASTIC

running from my hair, down my soaked uniform and collecting in an ever-expanding puddle on the floor.

'Cunners is his neighbour,' Ag added with a *tremor* in her voice.

'Even more fantastic. Do you think legumes need a category of their own?' Ag offered to take me home and hang with me there. 'Are you **kidding**?' I said. 'Have you seen the **state of this pantry**?' They really didn't want to leave my side, but I told them the party needed it's hosts so they should get out there! They knew there was **NO CHANGING MY MIND** because hey, they're my **best friends**. They hugged me, squeezing my soggy clothes without flinching, and left. **Cheesey-cheeses!** I knew if they hugged me I'd start crying. I wiped away my tears. There was no time for **crying**. There were noodles to be dewey decimalised.

THE UN-ROMANTIC MOVIE . . .

'Hey,' he said sending a **shudder down my spine.**

I can't let him see I've been crying, don't turn around, Tracy, whatever you do.

'Hey,' I said, continuing with the noodles. **BOMO didn't get the hint** and launched into his story/excuse. I wanted to **CONCEPT HUG** him so badly. It would be just like in the movies: I would say, 'I'm sorry, it was me,' and he would say, 'No, it's me.' And then the credits would roll and people would wipe away the **tears of happiness** knowing the **TWO PEOPLE MOST RIGHT FOR EACH OTHER** were finally together.

But even from his opening line, I knew this was not going to be that kind of movie. Our movie was more of an un-romantic comedy, which went a little like this . . .

INT. KITCHEN—PANTRY—DAY

[Tracy continues to file noodles using the dewey decimal system as her guide. She ignores the obvious puddle on the floor and brushes her damp, lifeless hair from her eyes. BOMD is trying desperately to engage her in conversation.]

> BOMD
>
> Tracy, you have to understand, I moved from interstate and I'm going to a new school. I want to fit in.

> TRACY
>
> Uh-huh.

[Tracy moves onto sorting the pasta.]

BOMD

Cunners is my mate, he's my neighbour,
he's showing me the ropes and he said
you were . . . anyway, I wanted to
look cool and I was worried about what
everyone would think. You would too,
right?

TRACY

Yep, been there done that.

BOMD

We can still be friends. I still like
you.

[Tracy whirls to face BOMD, trying to hide
her anger.]

TRACY

Oh, so everything that happened
before, that was you liking me?

BOMD

Yes. Oh thank goodness
you get it.

TRACY

Oh I get it, loud and
clear.

BOMD

Great, because what
we can do is keep our
friendship secret so I still look cool
and make cool friends. We pretend we
don't know each other while we're at
school. But out of school, we can hang
out . . . so long as no-one knows.

TRACY

That is such a great idea!

BOMD

You are the coolest chick ever.

TRACY

I know. But you are even cooler
because you have just shown me what an
idiot I've been.

BOMD

What? I thought you understood—

TRACY

Oh I do . . . now.

BOMD

I don't understand.

TRACY

I didn't think you would, so I'm going
to explain. No matter how cool you
try to be and no matter how much you

act like someone you're not, there's
probably going to be a person somewhere
who doesn't even like the pretend-y you.

                    BOMD

I still don't get it.

                    TRACY

Mmm, unfortunate because you need to.
See, I've road-tested the pretend-y
Tracy. It was really hard work trying
to be someone I'm not. And I did it to
try and impress people like you. But
today I found out that some things are
just out of your control . . . like
other peoples' behaviour, even their
opinion of you and . . . puberty.

                    BOMD

Do you even understand what you're saying?

TRACY

Oh, I do and I'm going to make it crystal clear for ·you. I don't know if your little rules about our friendship would be something you would say to a guy. I doubt it, because you would  see him as your equal and wouldn't dare think a guy would need to 'obey' you. And maybe you think you can treat girls like you own them but you don't own me.

So you can take your rules on how I'm supposed to behave and the conditions of our friendship and you can . . . well, I'm not allowed to say the words

269

I'd like to say, so instead I'll say
this. Don't speak to me again until
you get your head around the fact that
I might be a girl but as a human, I am
your equal.

[Tracy storms out,
squelching as she goes.
BOMD shouting after her.]

SQUELCH!

            BOMD
So that's a no?

[FADE TO BLACK]

I AM A STORM TOO . . .

I STORMED out. OH BOMO!
My first concept boyfriend! I
stormed out, smack bang
into the entire party standing at
the door, having heard every
word I'd said. And you know
what, I didn't care! 'So obviously
you heard all that,' I said to my
audience.

So obviously you heard all that

SIDE-THOUGHT: Would a song and dance routine be a
good thing right now? Everyone's watching. No! Stop
it! No song and dance! END SIDE-THOUGHT

I continued my rant instead. 'Say what you want,
think what you want because I don't want to waste

another second worrying about whether people think I'm **cool** or **un-cool**. I'm pretty sure there's even rock stars with kids who think their **rock-star parents** are **UN-COOL**. And if you can be a rock star and your kids think you're un-cool then what are we worried about? That just popped into my head because I can't be bothered self-censoring because

I AM **TRACY LACY** AND I AM COMPLETELY COO-COO BANANAS.

I headed straight for the door ... when slowly, but then with **more gusto**, everyone started **clapping** ... and then **CHEERING!** Why would they do that? Why was this happening? There were only three possible answers to this question:

1. They'd spent their **entire holiday** worrying about the same thing.

2. They were so *relieved* someone else had finally said it for them.

3. Darn you, number three!

'I'm **not** a **Marcus**, I'm a **Ponky** and **I LOVE BEING** Ponky!' Ponky shouted to the crowd. Was this really happening? 'So what if the hairy man-boys think it's funny.' I grabbed Ponky in a hug while the guests chanted '**PON-KY! PON-KY! PON-KY!**'

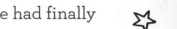
I have **one hair** on my chest ...

'I have one hair, does that make me a hairy man-boy?' Davin screamed over the noise.

VAROOOOOSH! Ag shot up from the depths of the pool causing everyone to leap about five metres in the air. In the name of **Be-jingie-jing-jing**, how long had she been there? 'You probably didn't notice me on the bottom of the pool. I go unnoticed a lot but it **doesn't bother me.** Oh, and my friends think I might be **part ninja.** I think they're right.'

This mind-reading thing had to stop but other than that all we could say was, 'We love you, Ag!' Then I grabbed Ponky by the hand and jumped into the pool. Along came the rest of the party in their best-quality school shoes and all. Hope those uniforms don't shrink, otherwise we were all in **BIG** trouble.

SPLISH SPLASH . . .

We might have been heading to high school in a couple of days but right now we were behaving like a bunch of out-of-control toddlers. There were water fights, dunkings, waterbombs, belly-whackers, it was on and it was so much fun until . . .

AARRRRRGGGGHHH!

came the ear-piercing scream. There, for all to see, bobbing down the middle of the pool, was a small, brown, log-shaped object. It took but a moment to work out what it was.

'CODE BROWN! CODE BROWN! EVERYONE OUT OF THE POOL!' I ordered.

But they were already out, except for Leif. 'Relax. It's the inside of **a sausage roll.** The pastry's fallen off, is all.' Then he ate it. The **HORRIFIED HORRIFICATION** on Leif's face might have been caused by the sausage meat being soaked in chlorine, or it might have been because **it wasn't** a sausage roll **missing its pastry** after all. I guess we'll never know and frankly **I don't want to.**

♡ **1** day to the start of **HIGH SCHOOL**

NO WORDS REQUIRED . . .

Me, Ag and Ponky sat staring out the window of **THE LOUNGE (DA-DA DA DAAAAA!)**. It was becoming one of our **favourite haunts** because we knew we wouldn't be disturbed . . . unless there was a sudden

need for a 'family talk' because Grandma turned up with a pav or something.

Outside, summer rain poured down, washing away all that didn't belong, leaving that which did, sparkling and new. It was nice.

'So, does this mean OBULOG is over?' Ponky asked.

'I don't know,' I answered honestly. 'I think if something you do makes you unhappy, you should change it. But changing to impress someone, I'm not so sure about that.'

'So, do we just accept who we are?' Ag asked.

'I think that's the idea but apparently there's this thing called the "HUMAN CONDITION" and it sometimes

makes it hard for us to do that. It was in the one-and-a-half self-help books I read.'

'Do you think this "𝐇𝐔𝐌𝐀𝐍 𝐂𝐎𝐍𝐃𝐈𝐓𝐈𝐎𝐍" will be a problem at high school?' Ponky asked.

'I hope not because I don't even know what it means.'

The rain grew heavier. We watched the droplets of water racing each other down the window pane. Some found an easy path. Others were blockaded, stopped in their tracks. 'Maybe,' I said, 'we need to be a bit more like the rain drops. The ones that win the race go with the flow.'

'And maybe if you get stuck, like the other raindrops, you just keep trying until you find a way around whatever's stopping you,' said Ponky.

'And even if you take the wrong path, that's better than not taking any path at all,' Ag said.

'And sometimes you can't control stuff. You've just gotta let go . . . like the raindrops.' I added, before quickly recalling 'The Areas of Improvement List', the thing that started this whole journey. Specifically point 4, always wanting the last word. **WHAT IS WRONG** **WITH ME?** 'Could someone please say something?' I begged.

Ponky reached out and took my hand, Ag took the other. There was nothing left to say.

THE NIGHT BEFORE THE BIG DAY . . .

As I packed my school bag, ready for the big day, I thought about stuff . . . and then more stuff. Yes, I was scared about going to high school, but I was excited too. And I'm pretty sure everyone else felt the same way.

I remembered back to when I was so worried about fitting in and all that. When my mum told me I walked to the beat of a different drum, I thought she was giving me a hint, telling me if I wanted to fit in, just march to the same beat and it will all be OK. Now I realise Mum was actually giving me a compliment, in her 'no-frills-mum-ism' kind of way. I know what she really meant was being different is good, get over it, accept it, move on. (She's really not good at expressing emotions.)

And if there's one thing the summer holidays have shown me, it's that I'm not good at 'being the same'. I'm much better at being me, 'completely coo-coo bananas Tracy Lacy'.

My uniform had been rehemmed, though Mum did make a comment about how the purple stripe seemed to have **faded**. (Thank you chlorine gods.)

And I packed my ballet bag. After a six-week break from ballet class I **couldn't wait** to get back to it. There's something I've **NEVER TOLD ANYONE**, not even Ag and Ponky, because it sounds a bit 'deep' and 'poetic' but I'm not trying to be. It's just that when I'm **dancing**, gliding across that floor, the music takes me somewhere else and I think that somewhere else is the closest I ever get to being **TRULY ME. See, pukesville**.

Oh well, this is it . . . my final sleep before I pass through the gates to Northwood High.

Morning, twinkle toes. Oh and good luck today. If you survive, great, if not, what song do you want played at your funeral?

Oh, how funny. By the way, I told Mum you wanted a sausage roll for lunch.

T-minus **0** days to the start of **HIGH SCHOOL**

THIS IS IT!

We're in our first assembly . . . the most **boringest boring thing** I've had to endure, so I'm sneaking a quick diary entry. Aside from assembly, it all went **GREAT** this morning. Me, Ag and Ponky stood at the Northwood High gates, just as we had way back at the end of primary school.

'There is one thing I think we need to shake on,' I said.

'Oh no, if this is another giant, self-improvement project . . .' Ponky protested.

It wasn't. It was really quite simple.

'I just want us to have **each other's backs**. Always and always!' I said.

'But we do,' Ag said.

'Goes without saying,' Ponky added.

'Can we just shake on it, so it's like our own first day ceremony thing?' We put our hands on top of each other's.

'**Always and always!**' we said.

Look out for
the next book:

For Classy Captain

Coming in 2017